1/9/12

Look out for the other
CODENAME **QUICKSILVER** books

The Tyrant King

Burning Sky

Killchase

Adrenaline Rush

End Game

CODENAME
QUICKSILVER

In the Zone

Allan Jones

Orion
Children's Books

With special thanks to Rob Rudderham

First published in Great Britain in 2012
by Orion Children's Books
a division of the Orion Publishing Group Ltd
Orion House
5 Upper St Martin's Lane
London WC2H 9EA
An Hachette UK company

1 3 5 7 9 10 8 6 4 2

A catalogue record for this book is available from the British Library.

ISBN 978 1 4440 0545 5

Printed in Great Britain by Clays Ltd, St Ives plc

For Amber, without whom . . .

CHAPTER **ONE**

Zak Archer was about to give up searching for his friend in the old factory building when he heard a scuffling sound from above. He glanced up in time to see something large and heavy plummeting towards him from one of the steel gantries.

He jumped back with a startled yell. The thing hit the concrete floor with a sickening thud. Zak stumbled, his heart thundering.

The thing was Spizz. He lay there, all twisted and wrong; his head at an unnatural angle, his face towards Zak, his eyes open but blank. A trickle of blood ran from his mouth.

Zak scrambled to his feet. His brain had stalled with the shock, but his body was on automatic. He stared at the contorted body of his dead friend, unable to take it in.

A spray can rolled from Spizz's torn backpack, rattling as it crossed the floor. Zak watched it in a blank daze.

He had come here to check that Spizz was okay. This was where his friend liked to hide out when he was in trouble. He'd guessed that Spizz had been picking pockets again – but he'd chosen his victim badly this time. That big blond-haired guy with the shark eyes Zak had seen chasing him through the crowded Games Arcade had looked dangerous. Vicious, even.

Another sound from above made Zak snap his head upwards.

Two men were hanging over the rail of the lofty gantry. The blond man and another – a man with bushy black hair and a pocked, red-skinned face that looked like day-old pizza.

A cold dread ran through Zak's body.

Had they chucked Spizz over the rail?

You don't kill people for picking your pocket.

The men looked down at him, their faces savage and ferocious.

Do you?

Blondie jabbed a finger at Zak as if he was throwing a dart. "Stay there, kid!" he shouted. The faces disappeared. Zak heard the echoing clang of running feet on the metal walkway. He glanced over to the angled steel stairway that would bring them straight to him.

Pain tightened in Zak's chest and he realized he wasn't breathing. He gasped in some air, his brain still scrambled.

Spizz gazed at him blankly like a broken doll.

Get out of here, you idiot! Haven't you figured it out? They *killed* me – and you're next.

Zak heard the clatter of feet on the stairs. They were coming for him.

Fear kicked in and he lurched away from the dead body, blundering over the rubbish and lumps of scrap metal that were scattered over the floor. He raced between the rusting hulks of big old machines, dodging past the sharp edges – running for his life.

The walls of the abandoned factory were covered in the same spray-painted words – over and over again in a rainbow of different colours.

SPIZZ! SPIZZ! SPIZZ ROOLS! SPIZZ ROCKS! SPIZZ!

Spizz had always liked to leave his mark.

As he ran, Zak glimpsed his reflection in a sheet of steel – beneath the stiff spray of his gelled brown hair, his face was twisted in terror. He should never have come here. He should have minded his own business.

Spizz, you mental case! What have you got me into?

He heard Blondie give a yell. "Don't make me have to chase you, kid!" Zak looked over his shoulder in time to see Blondie leap down the last few steps of the stairway and come running after him. Pizza-face was two paces behind, heavier-built, snorting like a charging bull.

The two men were between Zak and the main entrance – but there was a smaller door in the far wall. He ran for it, leaping over the debris, zigzagging around the big machines.

He hit the door at full speed, barging into it with his shoulder, banging his hands down on the bar that held it shut. He reeled back, gasping in pain. The door was locked or jammed or something.

He was trapped. *Idiot!*

Blondie and Pizza-face slowed to a walk, like jackals with cornered prey. They were only about five metres away now.

"Don't be scared," Blondie called with a smile that cut his face open like a knife wound. "We're not going to hurt you."

Zak's heart banged against his ribs. His whole body was shaking.

Pizza-face moved away from Blondie, his beefy arms spreading to make it harder for Zak to dodge past them. "We just want to talk to you, kid."

"Talk about what?" Zak shouted, his eyes darting to and fro in search of some other way out. "Talk about why you killed Spizz?"

"You've got it all wrong, kid," said Blondie. And again came the razor-blade smile as he moved slowly forwards. "That's not how it happened."

Zak spotted something to his right. The windows all along the wall were divided into steel-framed sections and the lowest part of one window was open. The sill was about two metres from the floor and the gap that would lead to the outside was probably no more than thirty centimetres.

Tricky – but not impossible.

Zak pushed up the sleeves of the tatty and stained old anorak he was wearing. It was several sizes too big for him and he was only wearing it until he could hand it over to another of his friends.

He darted to the side, sprinting for the window. Pizza-face gave a howl of anger as he lurched after him.

Pushing down the fear, Zak focused on the narrow gap. It was full of blue sky. He would have one chance to get this right. He could hear the men's feet clumping on the concrete. Too close! One mistake, one misstep and they'd have him.

He made two long bounding leaps, gathering momentum – then he came down hard with both feet together and his knees bent. Pointing his arms above his head like a diver, he flexed his legs and aimed for the rectangle of sky.

He snatched hold of the metal sill with his fingers and jackknifed his arms, boosting himself through the slot. The lower lip of the window frame grazed his thighs and shins as he shot through the gap. His heels clicked on the upper lip and he was through. Tucking himself into a ball, he flipped his legs over and hit the ground rolling.

A couple of moments later he was on his feet again, his lungs pumping air, his heart raging in his tight chest. Blood sang in his ears. His head spun with relief at his breakout. He looked back, and saw two angry faces at the window.

All those solitary hours of free running had paid off. He'd escaped.

"Yeah! How'd you like that?" he shouted, bouncing on his heels and punching the air. "Let's see you get through there, losers!" He felt angry and scared and defiant.

The faces vanished. They'd have to go all the way around to the main entrance now – he'd be long gone by the time they got out of there.

Then he saw something hit the window from the inside, smashing the frame, sending splintered glass flying. A broken office chair bounced past him as he threw himself away from the rain of glass fragments.

A moment later, Blondie was perched in the broken window frame. He jumped down. His eyes had become vicious slits and his face was ugly with frustrated rage.

Panicking, Zak spun around, already running, looking desperately for a way out.

A huge building site confronted him. This entire area was being torn down and redeveloped. On any other day, the whole place would have been swarming with workmen – but on a Sunday afternoon, it was quiet and still and empty of life.

Tower cranes made T shapes against the sky. Cement mixers and excavators stood idle. The portacabins were locked. Metal and plastic piping formed triangular heaps. Massed bags of cement rose like the battlements of an old castle.

A real obstacle course.

But Zak was good with obstacle courses.

The earth under his feet was scarred and furrowed by the tracks of heavy vehicles. The ground sloped down to a tall chain-link fence with padlocked gates.

Zak ran for the fence. He glanced over his shoulder. The two men were close behind him – and they had murder in their eyes.

He ran faster, focusing on the rapidly approaching fence.

He heard shouting behind him.

Now he was running full tilt at the fence, springing high, catching hold of the wire with both hands and the toes of both feet. He used his speed to bound up to the top. He folded his legs under him, balancing for a moment on the unsteady fence before launching himself into the air on the far side.

Bracing himself, he landed well on all fours, propelling himself onward with hands and feet.

He ran on, glancing around. He had expected to see the two men staring at him in amazement through the chain links. But Blondie was already at the top of the fence and even thickset Pizza-face was halfway up the far side.

These guys were in good shape.

Zak jinked to the right and sprang onto a big stack of cement sacks. Grey dust spouted into the air as he ran along the top of the stack and leaped across to a triangular pile of long yellow piping. Spreading his arms for balance, running with one foot directly in front of the other, he sped along the ridge of pipes as they creaked and shifted under him.

But Blondie was no slouch. Zak saw him racing alongside the stack of pipes, keeping pace with him.

A wooden plank led from the far end of the heap of pipes, stretching across to a hump of raw earth. And from there it was just a short run to a brick wall and the buildings beyond.

Zak risked another look back as he hit the plank. Blondie and Pizza-face were still close on his tail, running hard.

Zak sprinted along the plank and went careering down the slope of hard-packed earth, heading for the wall. Two metres? Easy.

He was up and over it in a flash. There was a longer drop on the far side, maybe four metres down into a narrow alleyway that ran between the wall and some kind of tall office building. He hesitated a moment then made the jump. It jarred him, but he knew how to flex his legs to absorb the impact.

Then he realized his mistake. He turned. To the left the alley led to a dead end. A metal door blocked the exit in the other direction. There were no doors in the wall of the building, and the only windows were high out of reach.

There was no way out.

Zak heard a panting grunt. Blondie was on the top of the wall. He was grinning as he jumped down.

"Fast but not too smart, eh, kid?" Blondie said, and suddenly there was a long serrated hunting knife in his fist. He moved forwards, his eyes glittering.

"Let's get this over with."

CHAPTER **TWO**

Zak jumped back, keeping a distance between himself and Blondie. The knife flashed in the sunlight. Pizza-face appeared at the top of the wall, scarlet-cheeked, sweating and blowing. He threw a leg over and lowered himself to the ground.

"Wrong place, wrong time, Speedy Gonzales," he spat, lumbering towards them.

Zak was terrified, but he wasn't finished. These murderers were *not* going to get him, not like they'd got Spizz. He'd seen one slim opportunity to get himself out of that hole. He spun around and raced for a pair of big dumpsters that stood at the blind end of the alley. He sprang onto the nearest dumpster and jumped up to grab a drainpipe that ran under a small window. The window was divided in two and one side was open.

Quick as an eel, Zak was through the window. Now he found himself in a washroom with big steel sinks and piles of towels and mops and buckets. The door leading out was unlocked. He flung himself into a corridor and slammed the door behind him. He felt a little giddy, as if he'd just stepped off a white-knuckle ride.

The long empty corridor stretched in both directions. There were double swing doors at either end. Now if he could get down to ground level and find an open door, he'd be home free!

He ran along the corridor and pushed through the swing doors. Stairs led up and down. He took the stairs down four at a time. Things were all too raw and terrible for him to feel pleased with himself – but the relief at having escaped stamped a wild, fixed grin on his face.

And then he came to the exit and found it blocked by a steel shutter. The grin vanished. Frustrated, Zak hammered on the shutter with both fists. It rattled and clanged, but it would take more than fists to shift it. Doors led left and right, but they were locked. There was another pair of swing doors and more stairs that went down to the basement — that was no use to him. He wanted out!

He paused, forcing himself to calm down and think for a moment. If he went back up again, he might find an open window on the street side of the building.

At least he had time to consider his options now he'd left Blondie and Pizza-face stranded in that alley.

A noise from above proved him wrong. Blondie was staring down the stairwell at him. The man gave a yell of frustrated anger as Zak kicked through the swing doors and raced along another corridor, trying every door as he went.

They were all locked.

The boom of doors bursting open echoed along the corridor and Zak spun around to see Blondie again.

Unbelievable!

This guy was like the Terminator.

Panic welled up. Zak felt himself losing control.

He spotted a couple of steel-framed chairs and a small table up against the wall. He snatched at one of the chairs and spun it around, releasing it to go bouncing along the corridor.

Yes!

Blondie was moving too fast to avoid it. He tried to jump, but the chair caught him on the knee and he crashed to the floor.

Zak didn't wait to see how badly he'd hurt the man. He didn't care. He shouldered his way through more swing doors and hit another stairwell. He went up the stairs in great leaps, arms swinging, chest heaving, gulping in air. He came to the landing just as Pizza-face burst through another set of swing doors right behind him.

But Zak had found his rhythm now. It was something that happened when he was running – a moment when the gears in his brain and body seemed to mesh and he suddenly felt as though he could outrun the wind.

Zak lunged to the side as the big man grabbed for him. He twisted in mid-air, striking his feet off the wall and darting past Pizza-face so that he was halfway up the next flight of stairs as the red-faced man was still grabbing for where he'd been a split second before.

Three flights up, he ran out of floors. A final, narrow concrete set of stairs led to a grey metal door. The roof, maybe?

Zak scrambled up the stairs and yanked down hard on the door handle. It gave suddenly and he tumbled forwards, sprawling on to a wide flat roof under a scorching sun.

He was on his feet again in an instant.

Apart from the brick-built block with the door in it,

Zak couldn't see any obvious way off the roof. Maybe there was a fire escape ladder or something?

He ran across the roof. Nothing.

He heard the clang of the steel door being barged open. Blondie and his knife were on the roof. But he was limping now. He must have hurt his leg somehow. Aww! Shame!

Beyond a gulf of empty air, Zak saw the rooftop of another building.

Taking long deep breaths, he sprinted hard, his eyes fixed on the far roof.

He lifted himself. His leading foot came down a final time on the raised edge of the roof. He pushed off into space. There was a deep, yawning trench of nothingness under him. The wind rushed in his ears. The blood pounded in his temples. He felt exhilarated. Focused.

Zak landed awkwardly on the far roof, twisting his ankle and crashing over and over on the hot tarmac. He came to a bone-jarring halt up against the brick trim of a sloping skylight, gasping for breath, hurting all over, winded and dizzy. But he'd made it.

His ankle was on fire. It wasn't a serious injury – he knew that from past experience – but it would slow him down. Long enough for Blondie to make the same leap with that big knife in his paw.

Zak sat up, resting his back against the brickwork, and looked across to where Blondie stood balancing on the edge of the far rooftop. The knife flashed sunlight. Blondie looked over at Zak, as though weighing up his chances. He was favouring his right leg. Maybe he wouldn't be able to make the jump after all.

A few tense seconds passed. Zak was about to get to his feet when Pizza-face arrived.

"Get over there," Blondie ordered.

Pizza-face leaned over the edge of the roof. He gave Blondie a dubious shrug.

"The kid did it – you can do it," Blondie snapped. "Go!"

Tightening his lips to a thin white line, Pizza-face backed away. Blondie stared at Zak and a slow smile twisted his mouth. He raised the knife towards Zak and made a swift, sideways slashing movement across the air. My knife – your throat. Any minute now.

Zak felt sick.

He watched as Pizza-face came running up to the roof edge and launched himself off.

He's going to make it. I'm dead.

But halfway across the gap, it was obvious Pizza-face wasn't going to make it after all. He lost momentum, his arms and legs flailing, his face twisted with fear and despair. He smacked into the top of the wall, one hand

and one elbow catching hold of the raised edge, his expression exploding into agony.

Without thinking, Zak scrambled forwards, reaching out to help him. A crazy thing to do, really – it just felt instinctive to try and save the guy from falling if he could. He'd worry about the consequences later.

But the elbow slipped off the wall and the terrified face vanished. For a moment, Zak saw the white fingers clinging on. Then they were gone.

There was a horrible silence.

Strange. In movies people always yelled when they fell to their deaths.

Arrrrrgggggghhhhhhhhhh . . . Splat!

Pizza-face didn't make a sound.

Zak moved to the edge of the wall and peered down. A dark lump stained the grey tarmac below.

Zak didn't feel sorry for him. A bit sick maybe, and pretty disgusted by the gruesome way the man had died. But his horrible death had been payback for what had happened to Spizz. It had served him right.

He looked across to where Blondie was standing. The man's face was set and hard. Cold blue eyes glittered.

A kind of terrified defiance blazed through Zak. "Come and get me, then!" he shouted. "Any time you're ready."

Blondie looked at him venomously for a moment,

then turned and limped back across the rooftop towards the door.

Zak had the feeling that this wasn't over.

Zak made his way along the narrow road that ran beside the railway arches under Waterloo Station. Rubbish was piled up against the black brickwork and scraps of old newspaper rolled and floated in the breeze. The road was sometimes used as a rat run by taxi drivers, but mostly it was home to a ragged scattering of street people.

His ankle ached still, but the immediate pain had quickly worn off and he wasn't even limping as he entered the shadowy underworld of the forgotten and unwanted people of London.

A skylight and a helpfully open window had been Zak's way out of the office building. But, all the way here, he'd been looking over his shoulder, expecting at any moment to see Blondie again. He felt sick and headachy and he just wanted to be somewhere quiet so he could lie down and recover from his ordeal.

Spizz hadn't been a close mate for some time, but Zak had never seen a dead body before, and thinking about those frozen, open eyes gave him the shakes. And those two guys wanted to do the same to him. What had he stumbled into?

But before he went home, there was someone he needed to see. Someone he could talk to about what had happened.

He found the arch he was looking for and walked into the deep cool darkness under the old Victorian brickwork. Makeshift beds and rusty supermarket trolleys and bags of strange personal stuff lined the walls of the arch. One or two bodies were huddled there, but Zak guessed that most of them were off hunting for food or compassion.

He came to an elaborate construction of hardboard and wooden slats and plastic sheeting. A ragged blanket served as a door. He tapped his fingers on the hardboard roof.

"Dodge? You in there?" he called. His friend had three or four boltholes around the city, but this was kind of his base camp.

A deep gravelly voice responded from within. "Who comes a'calling?"

Zak gave the usual response. "A wayfaring stranger, Dodge."

"Welcome, stranger." The blanket was thrown back. "What have you got for me, Zachary? What exotic cargoes do you bear? Sandalwood and cinnamon and sweet white wine?"

A thin man in a ruinous pinstripe suit looked out at him, his face half hidden by a long black beard, his sunken eyes bright with intelligence under bushy brows. The wreckage of boots covered his feet, held together with string and duck tape.

He was the only person in Zak's life who called him Zachary. Zak had known him for a couple of years now, ever since Zak had offered him half a sandwich one chilly winter afternoon on Waterloo Bridge. The thing about Dodge was that he never made judgements and he never told Zak what to do. Zak could be angry or fed up or frustrated or confused, and Dodge would just listen to him while he talked. There were no other adults in Zak's life who did that. Everyone else had an agenda. Dodge was just a pal.

Zak dropped to his knees and the man moved aside to let him in. It smelled in there, but Zak was used to it. An open tuna tin and another of baked beans were the remnants of Dodge's lunch.

"No poetry today, Dodge," Zak said wearily. "I've got stuff I have to tell you." He looked into Dodge's dark eyes. "Really horrible stuff, Dodge. I don't know how . . . I can't really . . . it was . . ." He paused.

Dodge's hand rested on his shoulder. "Start at the beginning," he said gently. "Carry on till you get to the end, and then stop."

"I was coming to see you," Zak began hesitantly. "Paul from the home was going to throw this out." He plucked at the big anorak. "I rescued it. I thought it would do you."

"Very nicely." Dodge nodded. "It can be cold under here – even in July."

"I stopped off on the way to play some games at the arcade. I was minding my own business when Spizz came barging into me like an elephant – he nearly knocked me over."

Dodge frowned. "Spizz? The boy with the Michelangelo aspirations?"

Zak stared blankly at him.

"Always painting walls," Dodge explained, miming spraying paint.

"Yes. That's him. He was running away from this big blond guy." Horror filled Zak's eyes as he remembered the look on Blondie's face. "I thought he must have tried picking the guy's pocket. Anyway – Spizz legged it with the other guy running after him. I carried on playing for a bit, then I thought I'd go check if Spizz had got away okay. He usually hides out in an empty factory off

Sumner Street." Zak swallowed hard. "I went in there, Dodge . . . and . . . and . . ."

Slowly, piece by dreadful piece, Zak told his friend everything that had happened on that impossible Sunday afternoon.

CHAPTER **THREE**

Dodge's voice was clipped and precise. "Are you absolutely certain that Spizz was dead? Not just knocked unconscious?"

Zak shook his head, remembering his friend's glazed eyes. "He was dead," he said, startled to find he was trembling. "And they were going to kill me, too, Dodge. I know they were." His voice broke. "Who were they? What was it all about?"

"You think Spizz stole from them?" Dodge asked.

"I guess so. What else?"

"What else, indeed." Dodge's thick brows came down,

almost hiding his eyes. "If that's the case, your friend picked the wrong pocket, Zachary," he said. "My guess is he fell foul of some professional villains."

"But why chase *me*?" Zak asked. "What did I do?"

"You were a witness, Zachary," Dodge said solemnly. "You saw what they'd done. They couldn't risk you going to the Old Bill." Dodge looked sharply at Zak. "That's what you have to do, Zachary. Tell the police. You know that, don't you?"

"I can do that right now," Zak said, feeling in his pocket for his mobile phone. In the panic of the chase, he'd almost forgotten he had it on him. It was only a basic one – no Internet access or games apps or anything cool like that.

"Try to remember every detail," Dodge told him. "Especially about the blond man. Picture him in your mind. Face, age, hair, eye colour. What he was wearing. How he spoke. His accent. Everything – while it's all still fresh in your memory."

Zak scrambled out of the hardboard hovel that Dodge called home. "Thanks, Dodge, I'll do that." He took two steps before he remembered again why he'd been coming to visit his friend in the first place. He shrugged off the big old anorak. "For you – to keep warm at night."

Dodge took it. "Thank you kindly, young Zachary." He smiled. "In charity there is no excess." His eyes became grave. "Call the police!"

"Yes, I will." Zak jogged to the end of the arch with the phone in his hand. He pressed out three nines.

A woman's voice answered. "Emergency Call Centre. Which service do you require?"

"Police, please," Zak said as he walked along to the main road.

"I'm connecting you now. Please wait a moment."

Zak stopped before he hit the busy main road – there was a lot of traffic roaring past and pedestrians crossing to and fro. No one came down this little street, though. He sometimes found it weird that the normal world and Dodge's hidden world could be so close to one another and yet so far apart.

"Police emer—" The man's voice cut off mid-word. There were a series of clicks then the voice of a different man spoke. "Police emergency. How can I help you?"

"Listen, you have to believe what I'm going to tell you," Zak said. "Someone's been murdered, okay? His body's in the old factory off Sumner Street. Two men did it – but one of them is dead. The other one's got a knife. He's really dangerous."

"Okay, son, I'm listening," the voice said calmly. "Tell me your name and give me all the details you can, please."

Zak spilled the story in a gush of tumbled words. He wasn't sure how much sense he was making. He felt like running down the street screaming.

"Now listen to me, son," said the voice when he had finished. "I'm going to arrange for a police car to be sent to the factory. Now then, are you at home?"

"No, not really. Not at all. I'm out." Zak felt as if his brain had been through a blender. This was all getting too much. Way too much.

"Okay – listen, Zak. You need to get home, right now. Will your parents be in?"

"I don't have parents, I live in a children's home. Robert Wyatt House in Lychgate Street, London SE1."

"That's fine – you're doing fine, Zak. I want you to go straight back there now for me, okay? I'm going to send a police car to your place of residence. You're going to have to make a statement. It's nothing to worry about."

"Fine. I can do that."

"Great. You sound like a smart kid, Zak. I'm going to hang up and get things moving. You've done really well. You go home, right?"

"Right." There was a click and the phone went dead.

Zak pushed the phone into his jeans pocket and stepped out into the noise and bustle of the main road.

The blond-haired man smiled as he tapped his Bluetooth to end the call. He was squatting on a low seat in the back of a black transit van.

Convincing. Very convincing. He'd even changed his voice just in case the kid recognized it.

The interior of the van glowed with the bluish light of a series of computer screens set side by side on a fixed metal workstation. There was a keyboard and a small oblong device that blinked red lights and fed cables into and out of a row of desktop computer towers.

A mobile phone sat on the worktop – connected to the blinking device. It was face up, but if the man had turned it over, it would have showed the word SPIZZ carefully painted along the back. The blond man had taken it from Spizz a few seconds before he'd tipped him over the rail. He didn't want it getting broken in the fall – it might come in handy. In the end it had turned out to be more useful than he'd expected. It had helped him to track down that light-footed little street rat.

They'd searched the pickpocket Spizz when they'd caught him on the gantry, but the thing he'd stolen wasn't on him. The only other person he'd had any contact with was the smart-mouthed kid. The blond man remembered him from the arcade. Spizz must have passed it to him there. That was the only answer.

The man picked up a BlackBerry and speed dialled a number.

Someone answered immediately.

"It's me," said the blond man, leaning back and stretching his aching leg as much as he could in the confined space. "Yes – it worked fine. I got his number off the dead kid's phone. I used the new gizmo to hack in and I intercepted him making a call to the police." He gave a jagged smile. "He lives at Robert Wyatt House, Lychgate Row, SE1. It's some kind of children's home. I've just sent him back like a good little doggy. Now get yourself over there and deal with him!"

A tap on his earpiece cut the call dead.

The blond man sat quietly for a few moments, rubbing his knee and looking at the computer screens. Then he heaved himself up and pushed out of the van. He slammed the back doors and limped around to the driver's seat.

"Little rat!" he hissed as he climbed in. His knee was giving him trouble. He turned the key and the engine growled. The man frowned as he steered out of the side

34

street. "Dead little rat!" he said, and the crooked grin was back on his bony face. "Dead little street rat!"

Zak was whacked. Zonked. Shattered. All he really wanted was to crawl into bed and pull the covers over his head. But he was almost home. The street he was in fed into Lychgate Street right opposite the front entrance of the children's home. But before he would be allowed to crash out, he knew he had to tell his story. To the residential social workers, Kath and Paul. To the police. To Spizz's mates.

He wished he didn't have to do that. He wished none of this had happened.

All the way home he kept seeing Spizz's dead eyes in his head. He couldn't shake the image of him lying on the factory floor.

He could see the grand entrance to Robert Wyatt House now. There was a stone portico and five stone steps that led up to the wide doorway. Rich people had lived there in the old days. Now the local council owned it and it was full of orphaned kids.

As Zak came to the corner, he saw a black transit van pull up. Two men in dark suits got out. The police? No uniforms, though – CID? Flying Squad?

Zak had come up against the police a few times in the past – and not in a good way. But that had been three years back, before he'd realized that Spizz's big plans always led to disaster.

The two men mounted the steps to the entrance.

Zak was about to step into the open when a hand came over his mouth from behind and something small and hard jabbed between his shoulder blades.

For a moment Zak was too startled to be scared – then he remembered Blondie's knife and his body went cold with fear.

"Hands up, Zachary!" hissed a voice. A young female voice. The thing was shoved more forcefully into his spine. Not a knife. Blunt.

A *gun*?

"*Hands . . . up!*" The voice was fiercer this time. "Not a word, or you're finished. Got me?"

Zak nodded and lifted his arms. The two plain-clothed police officers were at the door of the Home. One of them pressed the entryphone.

The hand moved from his mouth. He felt something being drawn tight around his chest – a belt of some kind. He heard the clink of metal on metal. His arms were wrenched down and held to his sides, as the girl pressed close to his back.

There was a whirring sound. The belt jerked up under his arms, wrenching him and lifting him off his feet.

He gave a gulp as the air was squeezed out of his lungs. He looked down and saw that the pavement was rapidly falling away beneath them.

They twisted slowly in the air as they rose higher, the girl gripping him with one looping arm, her breath on his neck, the belt biting under his armpits.

Whirrrrrr.

The ground was now nine or ten metres below Zak's slowly revolving trainers.

Suddenly the whirring stopped. Zak felt the girl shift her weight. There was a pull to one side. His legs struck against the wall of the building. The girl moved away from him, and then he was dragged unceremoniously over a windowsill and into a room like a fish being hauled out of the sea.

He lay on his front on bare floorboards that smelled of dust and decay. The belt around his chest was loosened. He could breathe properly again.

Blood hammered in his head. What was coming?

A bullet?

What?

Utterly bewildered, he turned over and sat up.

The girl was at the window, unclamping a small

metal box from the frame. Thin wires coiled from the device, attached to a webbing strap. It was some sort of powerful winch, Zak guessed.

He was relieved to see that there was no sign of a gun.

But what the heck . . . ?

The girl pushed the box into a backpack that lay under the window. She turned and looked at him.

She couldn't have been much more than a year or two older than he was, Zak guessed. She was tall and very thin, all legs, with a long face and black hair pulled into a ponytail. She was wearing black tights and a short dark skirt and top.

She was kind of good-looking, he thought, although her eyes were dark and ferocious – like the eyes of a predatory bird – and her expression was grim.

"Those guys are not the police," she told him. "Trust me on this. If they get their hands on you, you'll be found floating down the Thames with your legs tied around your neck." She stepped towards him, moving gracefully, like an athlete. Zak pushed himself away from her across the bare floor.

Trust me? She had to be kidding!

She smiled and offered a hand. "C'mon. I don't bite," she said. "I just rescued you from some bad juju, Zachary. Those guys are dangerous."

She advanced on him, still offering her hand.

Reluctantly, Zak took it and she pulled him to his feet with an unexpected strength. Skinny but power-packed, he realized.

He stared at her. "What do you want?" he demanded. "Who are you? What was that thing?" He gestured to the backpack. "How did it *do* that?"

"It's called a zipper," she said. "It works on xenon fluoride batteries." Her eyes narrowed. "We don't have time for any more explanations right now. I have to get you away from here. If those guys find us, we're both dead meat, do you get that?"

The initial shock was wearing off now, and Zak's day had been bad enough without some loony girl messing with him. "I get that you're mental or something," he retorted. "And I'm not going anywhere with you." He looked around the empty room. The door was half open.

He had to get out of there. Quick.

Zak darted towards the door, hoping to catch the girl off guard and be away before she realized what was happening.

But he hadn't got more than three paces before she was on him. He hardly knew what was going on before she'd tipped him over and sent him crashing onto his face on the floorboards.

She came down on top of him, her knees in his back, her hands snatching his wrists and pulling his arms behind him – not enough to hurt, but enough to leave him struggling and unable to tip her off.

She leaned forwards, her mouth close to his ear. "Don't try that again," she warned. "It's a waste of effort." She gave his arms a sharp tweak. "Got me?"

"Yes . . . yes . . ." Zak gasped. "I get it . . ."

"Good. I'm going to get up now, and I'm going to take your arms to a safe place," she said sweetly. "It's your choice. Either you come along with your arms, or I take them on their own. What do you say, Zachary?"

"I'll come," Zak said.

What other choice did he have?

But something was nagging at him as he got to his feet.

How did this crazy girl know his name?

CHAPTER **FOUR**

"No more tricks," said the girl. "I need to check something out – then we're leaving."

Zak watched her warily as she padded across to the window. She crouched and rummaged in the backpack.

"How do you know me?" Zak asked.

"I looked you up," the girl replied. She was holding something that looked like a small pair of tapering binoculars with a long flexible cable sticking out from the front. She kneeled at the window, holding the binoculars to her eyes and twiddling knobs. The flexible cable extended out over the sill and twisted to the left and downwards.

"Oh, yes," she murmured. "That's them all right." She gestured to him. "Come on – see for yourself. Then maybe you'll believe me."

Zak went to her side. She handed him the strange binoculars. "Take a look through the snakescope," she said. "The buttons change the angle and focus."

He held the gadget to his eyes. A hugely magnified circle of wall filled his vision. He twisted the buttons and the wall went spinning away. There was some pavement. Another wall. A row of windows. The black transit van.

Amazing piece of kit!

I want one of these . . .

He turned the buttons more slowly. The magnified circle crawled up the steps of Robert Wyatt House. The two men were at the open door, talking to Paul. He couldn't see their faces, but one of them was very tall and had a sweep of silver-grey hair. Paul looked worried. But then Paul always looked worried.

"See?" the girl hissed, close to his ear. "That van isn't police issue. The Met use Vauxhall Zafiras. That's a Mercedes-Benz."

"So, who are they?" Zak asked.

"Foreign agents," said the girl.

Zak very nearly burst out laughing.

Foreign agents?

He gazed at her in disbelief, but she stared back. Deadly serious.

"They want something they think you have," she said. "They won't hesitate to kill you to get it."

Crazy!

"Whatever medication you're on – cut the dose," he said.

The corner of her mouth lifted with the hint of a smile. "Let me take you somewhere safe," she said. "Then I'll answer your questions. How does that sound?"

Zak shook his head. "I don't have anything foreign agents would be interested in," he said. "You've got the wrong person."

The girl's eyes burned into him. "Zachary Archer, fourteen years old, birthday 3rd of April, although that's only an educated guess. Found in a holdall as a baby outside St Thomas's Hospital. Mother and father unknown." She recited all this very rapidly, as though she were reading from a file. "Between the ages of four and ten, he was placed with five different sets of foster parents. None took. Friendly enough, but a bit of a loner and not good with discipline. Well above average school grades. Could do even better if he applied himself.

Favourite sport: long-distance running. Usually alone. Some problems with the police a few years back due to the bad influence of an older boy, Martin Spencer – also known as Spizz. Been a resident at Robert Wyatt House for four years and three months." She smiled again. "I've got the right person, Zachary. I know none of what's happening is your fault. I'm here to help you."

She took the snakescope from him and stuffed it into the backpack. She moved away from the window and stood up, slinging the pack over her shoulder.

"Coming?" she asked.

They walked rapidly through back streets. At every corner the girl paused and checked out the way ahead before moving on. If she saw people, she'd backtrack and find another route. All the while, Zak saw that she was consulting a kind of mobile phone – except that it wasn't like any phone he'd ever seen before. It was oval and silvery and almost as thin as a credit card.

Zak kept close, waiting for an opportunity to break the logjam of questions that was building up in his mind.

Who was she? How did she know so much about him? Where had she got those cool gadgets? The snakescope and the zipper – and that weird sci-fi phone. And what was that stuff about foreign agents? Did she mean spies? Were Blondie and Pizza-face *spies*? And if they were, why would they be after him?

The questions hammered inside his head, wanting out.

"Who are you?" he asked at last as they made their way along a narrow alley between high brick walls. He stopped in his tracks. The late afternoon sun was sinking and the alley was a well of shadows. "I want to know who you are right now, or I'm out of here."

She halted and turned. "Call me Rina," she said. "Will that do for now, Zachary?"

No, not really. Still – it was something.

"Can you do me a favour?" he asked.

Her eyes were flickering up and down the alley. "Name it," she said. "But be quick."

"Call me Zak – and tell me what's going on. How do you know me?"

"I was in the games arcade," Rina said. "Your friend stole my wallet." She moved from foot to foot, full of restless energy. "Walk and talk," she said. "It's not safe to stay in one place too long – not out in the open." She carried on down the gloomy alley. Zak followed.

"There's something in my wallet that those two men want," Rina's words came out machine-gun fast as she walked along the alley. "I think your friend Spizz passed the wallet to you when they started chasing him." She glanced at him. "How about you give it back?"

"He didn't give me anything," Zak said. "That never happened."

Rina gave him a sharp look. "I'm disappointed you don't trust me yet, Zak," she said. "Those men will stop looking for you once they know you've handed the thing over. Give it to me and you're off the hook. That's a promise."

"I have no idea what you're talking about," said Zak. "What makes you think Spizz gave me your wallet? I'm not his accomplice any more. Not for years."

"I followed you to that old factory," Rina said. "I got there shortly after you did." Her eyes were dark and hard on his. "I checked your friend's corpse, Zak. The wallet wasn't on him. Either they had it – in which case it was game over – or you had it, and I figured that as they were still chasing you, the wallet had to be with you."

"No," Zak breathed. "You've got it all wrong. They were chasing me because I saw them kill Spizz – not because I had your wallet." He stopped again. "And that still doesn't explain how you know all about me."

She turned again, angry now. "You're wasting too

much time with this!" she hissed. "If you'd just trust me—"

"Tell me the truth and I might," he retorted, refusing to back down.

"I frisked your dead friend," Rina said. "I found his wallet. It had his name and address in it." She held up the silvery disc. Zak could see a map on the screen. "This is called a Mob. It has Internet access. I used it to hack into the files at Robert Wyatt House. I scrolled through till I found your picture. I read your file. That's how I know about you – and that's how come I guessed you'd be heading home." Her eyes narrowed dangerously. "And that's how come I got to you before the men in the black Mercedes. A thank you for saving your life would be nice."

"Spizz didn't give me any wallet," Zak insisted. "I'd hand it over if he had. What do you think – I've got some kind of death wish?"

Rina looked at him dubiously – as if she was starting to believe him.

"He could have passed it to you without you realizing," she said. "When he crashed into you in the arcade. Have you checked your pockets?" Her eyes suddenly widened. "Where's the coat you were wearing?"

Zak stared at her – remembering that moment in the games arcade when the fleeing Spizz had crashed into him and almost taken him off his feet. It was true – Spizz could easily have slipped something into one of the pockets of the anorak. That old coat had been heavy – he wouldn't have noticed a little added weight.

"I don't have it," Zak said. "I gave it away."

"You did *what*?" For a split second Rina looked so ferocious that he took a step backwards. Then she made a visible effort to calm down. "Who did you give it to?" she asked.

A movement caught Zak's eye beyond her shoulder. A shape, slipping across the far end of the alley, moving from shadow to shadow. Seeing the sudden change in his eyeline, Rina spun around.

"Give it up, Rina," called a voice from the gloom. "You're done."

Rina's voice was like a whipcrack. "Switch!"

The hidden figure stepped from the shadows. It was a boy. He was about Rina's age, tall and muscular with close-cropped light brown hair and a wide-jawed, angular face. He bounced on his toes, knees flexed as he watched her. Even at that distance Zak could see his eyes gleaming like blue diamonds.

Give it up. You're done.

Zak stared at the newcomer in astonishment. Rina had been telling the truth – people were out to get her . . . and *him*! Crazy as it sounded – maybe he should have just believed her.

Rina moved so fast that Zak was left rooted to the spot. In an instant she was racing towards the boy – pulling the backpack from her shoulder and groping inside with one hand.

She pulled something from the bag. It looked to Zak like a torch, but when she aimed it at the boy, thin wires spun out from the end. The boy leaped to one side as the wires reached for him and missed. He bounced high with both feet, twisting his body and kicking off the wall, heading straight for her.

She flung the backpack at him but he fended it off in mid-air with his forearm.

The boy crashed into Rina and they both went spinning to the ground. But they were on their feet again in a split second, grappling together, each trying to throw the other down. After a brief struggle, they jumped apart, crouching low, arms spread, feet shifting constantly as they circled one another.

There was another flurry of movement. Rina kicked out, hooking her foot behind the boy's knee, trying to trip him. But he sprang over her scything foot and the missed blow unbalanced her. He came down again, snatching at her arm, pivoting on one heel, pulling her forwards and bending to the side so she was flipped over his hip, her ponytail and legs flying. She wrenched herself free and landed on her feet, facing him and ready for more. Then there were legs kicking out and punches flying faster than Zak could take in – forearms, knees and feet warding off the blows.

The boy was bigger than Rina, but she was so quick he couldn't land a punch or kick powerful enough to take her down.

They fought in focused silence, the only sounds being the gasp of their breath and the thud of blocked kicks and punches.

But fast as Rina was, Zak could see that the boy's additional weight and height were beginning to work for him. The end came suddenly. Rina hurled herself at him – he ducked and lunged forwards, his shoulder slamming into her abdomen. He straightened his legs, flipping her high.

She crashed onto her back on the hard ground and he was on her in an instant, his knees on her shoulders, his hands grabbing her wrists.

Her head turned towards Zak, her eyes pleading.

"Help me!" she gasped.

In a daze, Zak lurched forwards. He saw a length of rotten planking lying against one wall of the alley. He snatched it up and, stumbling towards the two fighters, brought it down across the boy's back.

The strip of decayed wood broke into pieces and the boy collapsed sideways with a low groan.

A moment later Rina was on her feet, panting and wild-eyed.

"I've killed him!" yelled Zak, hurling the remains of the plank away in horror.

Rina crouched at the boy's side. Her fingers felt his throat. "No you haven't," she said. "He's alive." She was on her feet again, snatching up her backpack. "They're closer than I thought," she said, reaching her hand for his. "We have to move – now!"

Zak grasped her hand and together they raced down the alley, leaving the boy lying in the dust.

CHAPTER **FIVE**

"Where are we going?" asked Zak as they zigzagged at a jog through a maze of backstreets and alleys. They had been on the move for some time now, but the girl seemed tireless. Zak was used to leaving people puffing in his wake, but she kept up with him step for step. Not that he was trying to outrun her – he could have kept this speed up all day long.

"We're going to ground," Rina panted. "I need to regroup."

"Who was he?"

Zak couldn't believe that he'd hit the boy. He wasn't

the violent type – not at all. He'd always avoided fighting if he could.

Rina didn't reply.

"This will do," she said a few moments later, pulling Zak into the sunken entrance of a boarded-up shop. The doorway was blocked with a plywood panel, chained and padlocked. She stood there for a moment, catching her breath. "Keep an eye out," she murmured.

He stared at her. "For what?"

"Anything."

He peered along the empty street. He had no idea what he was supposed to be looking for. Then he heard the rattle of chain behind him. A hand grabbed his wrist and he was yanked into a darkened hallway. Rina closed the door on them.

"How did you do that?" he asked. She had worked that padlock in a matter of seconds.

"Tricks of the trade," Rina said. "Upstairs. We can catch our breath now." She eyed him appraisingly. "Although you don't look like you need to."

He followed her up a staircase and into a room piled with old furniture and carpets. It smelled foul and the air was full of dust. Shafts of evening light filtered between the slats of the boarded-up windows.

Rina clambered over the junk to a window. She

stared out, her eyes narrowed and her face anxious. Zak watched as she moved from side to side, her body tense, examining the street from every angle.

"Who was that guy?" Zak asked. "What was all that about?"

Rina let out a long breath and sank to the floor with her legs folded up under her and her back to the wall. She looked silently at Zak for a long while, her eyes unreadable.

"This whole thing is totally insane," he said at last. "Why are we doing this? If those guys in the van were crooks or . . . *whatever* – we should call the cops." He pulled his phone out of his pocket. "I'm going to call them right now," he said.

"No."

"Then tell me what's going on!" Zak shouted, anger flaring suddenly. "I'm sick of this!"

She lifted her hands in a gesture that was almost like surrendering. "Okay," she said quietly. "I can't tell you everything, but I guess you deserve some kind of explanation." She beckoned. "Sit," she said. "Let's talk."

Zak moved closer and perched on a roll of carpet. The light streaked Rina's face with bands of black and white. He studied her, trying to figure her out.

"I work for a department of British Intelligence," she

began. "It's called Project 17. You won't have heard of it."

"You're kidding me," he blurted. "How old are you? Sixteen? And you work for British Intelligence?"

She sighed. "Yes," she said. "I do. My codename is Ballerina – Rina for short. I'm not going to tell you my real name."

"Of course not," Zak murmured sarcastically. "Top secret, I guess."

She gave him a sharp look. "If our enemies knew our real names they could come after our families, got it?" she said.

She sounded like someone fresh off a psycho ward – but then they *were* being hunted, he had to admit that. And how about those cool gadgets – not to mention her wicked fighting skills. You don't learn that kind of stuff at school.

But British Intelligence . . . ? *Really?*

He could still see Spizz lying twisted on the concrete floor. He could still see Blondie slashing the air with his big hunting knife. He could still see Pizza-face clutching hopelessly at the wall before he fell to his death.

And he could still see himself bringing the chunk of wood down on that boy's back.

"Project 17 is a branch of MI5," Rina continued. "Our remit is to counter foreign agents working in the

UK – international terrorists, organized international crime, all that – and anything else our bosses tell us." She paused for a moment, as though deciding what else she should tell him. "We work out of London, but our missions take us all over the world. We're all teenagers – that's the whole point. We're used for very special covert ops – where older agents might stand out. That guy who attacked me is called Switchblade . . ."

"Not his real name, I'm guessing," Zak broke in.

"No, not his real name," Rina replied. "He's a member of Project 17 – or I should say he *was* a member." Her eyes flashed. "He sold us out. He's gone over to the other side."

"What other side?" Zak asked.

"I'm not sure – a foreign agency . . . I don't know for what country yet – but I plan on finding out." Zak saw her hands tighten to white-knuckled fists. "He's smart . . ." she snarled. "Very smart. He knew I was onto him, so he framed me." Her shoulders shook with rage. "He managed to convince them all that I was the traitor! They were going to take me down. I had to run." She leaned towards him, her eyes shining with anger. "I have to get that memory stick to Colonel Hunter, Zak. That's the only way to clear my name."

Zak jerked back, startled by the vehemence in her

voice. "What memory stick?" he asked. Then it hit him. "There was a memory stick in your wallet!" he gasped. "The wallet that Spizz stole."

Rina nodded. "You're quick on the uptake, Zak," she said. "That's good. Switch downloaded a lot of secret information about us from our computers – everything a foreign power would want to know about Project 17. Code words, access points, personnel lists, mission archives, file data – the works. I caught him doing it. I knew there was something screwy going on, so I followed him. He left the memory stick in a drop box near Tower Bridge."

"A drop box?"

"It's a way for people to pass information without meeting up," Rina explained. "You arrange a time and place. Leave the thing. Your contact picks it up later. You never see him – he never sees you. It means there's no chain of people for anyone to follow."

Against his better judgement, Zak was beginning to believe her. Who would make all this stuff up? And it fitted with what had happened to Spizz.

Project 17. Teenage Secret Agents? Zak had the feeling he'd wandered through the looking glass at some point today. Thing was – how was he going to get back to the real world again?

"I waited till he'd gone, then I took the stick before it was picked up," Rina continued. "But Switch must have been watching. Next thing I know, I get a text from Hunter – our boss – telling me to get back to base straight away. I typed my codename into my Mob – I was gong to warn him about Switchblade. But the code had been erased. All my access codes had been wiped."

"Switchblade had already told your boss you were the traitor," said Zak.

Rina nodded. "Exactly," she said. "Then Switch called – he told me that Hunter had sent a Sweeper Team out after me."

"A Sweeper Team?"

"An armed clean-up squad," Rina explained. "They deal with serious problems – anything from sanitizing a crime scene to putting a bullet in someone's head and disposing of the body. They're not part of Project 17, but Hunter can call on them whenever he needs them."

"They were going to *kill* you?" Zak gasped. "Just like that? On Switch's say so?"

"Switch had been in the Project for three years – I was their newest recruit," said Rina. "Who were they going to trust?"

"All the same," said Zak. "I can't believe they'd just kill

you, without giving you a chance to explain. That's a bit harsh."

"They'd have taken me alive if they could," said Rina. "But without the memory stick, I had no proof to show Colonel Hunter. And your mate stole the stick when he lifted my wallet."

"So those two guys – the blond one and his mate – they were the Sweeper Team, right?"

Rina nodded.

"And the guys in the black van? They were the same?"

"Different team – same agenda," said Rina.

Zak leaned back, blowing his cheeks out. "Do you have any idea how crazy all this sounds?" he asked.

She gave a soft laugh. "Pretty crazy, I guess," she said. "But you know what they say about truth being stranger than fiction."

He looked at her thoughtfully. "I was really worried about that guy we left back there," he said. "I'm kind of glad I hit him now."

"Me too," Rina said and a wide grin spread across her face. "You're a good man to be with in a tight spot, Zak. Most other people would have run for the hills."

A good *man* . . .

Zak liked the sound of that.

"Just doing my job, ma'am." He mimicked the attitude

of a hundred cops in a hundred TV cop shows.

She laughed again. Then her face became serious. "Who'd you give the coat to, Zak?" she asked.

"A friend," Zak said. "I don't know his real name. He's kind of a tramp. He lives under the arches at Waterloo station. He calls himself Diogenes."

Rina nodded. "Cute," she said. "He named himself after Diogenes the Cynic – the Ancient Greek philosopher who lived in a barrel and begged for a living."

Zak stared at her in amazement – he only knew that because Dodge had told him. She was brainy as well as super-fit. Her cover story was getting more convincing all the time.

"People call him Dodgy-knees, or Dodge," Zak explained. "He's a really good guy – I help him out when I can. We have good talks." He frowned. "Paul at the Home was going to throw the anorak out – so I thought of Dodge."

"And you gave it to him," said Rina. "You're a good friend."

Zak shrugged. "So's he." He looked at her. "I don't want anything bad to happen to Dodge."

"It won't, trust me," said Rina. She stood up. "I just need the memory stick back, then you'll be done with me for ever." She smiled. "You'll never see me again

– that's a promise."

Zak was desperate to get all this over with, so it surprised him that he wasn't more thrilled by her promise.

Was there a tiny part of him that was actually enjoying the excitement?

Despite everything that had happened?

He got to his feet. "Okay," he said. "I'll take you to him."

CHAPTER **SIX**

It was evening by the time Zak and Rina arrived in the narrow street that led to the arches under Waterloo Bridge. Traffic still roared on the main road, and the streets swarmed with people.

The arches gaped like aching mouths. The shadows were thick and dark.

Zak glanced nervously over his shoulder. He was getting to be as edgy as Rina. There was a constant burning between his shoulder blades, as though the cross hairs of a rifle were aimed at his back.

And he had never realized how many black transit

vans there were on the streets. He must have counted a dozen or more on their way here.

The red glow of a fire played on the upper curve of Dodge's arch. Fingers of flame sprang from a metal bin. A woman bundled in shapeless clothes stood warming her hands.

"Hi, Esma," said Zak as he and Rina walked in under the arch.

The woman peered at him, shifting her feet, rubbing her cracked hands together. She nodded but said nothing.

Eyes gazed at them from the gloom; figures lay against the dank walls.

Zak led Rina to "The Mansion". That was what Dodge called his makeshift home.

He rapped on the hardboard roof with his knuckles. "Dodge? You at home?"

There was no reply. Zak stooped and pulled the blanket aside.

Dodge wasn't there. Neither was the anorak.

Zak turned. "Esma?" he called. "Seen Dodge at all?"

"Gone up west," she called back in a voice that croaked like a raven. She put a grimy finger under her nose, tilting it upwards. "Too good for the likes of us. Gone to have supper with the toffs."

"What does she mean?" Rina asked.

"He'll have gone to Soho – there's plenty of food to be had around the back of the restaurants – out of the bins, you know?"

Rina looked disgusted by the idea.

"Will he be back soon?" she asked Zak.

Zak shrugged. "No idea," he said. "It could be a while. He might be working the tourists. Dodge says that tourists are a good target for small change." He didn't add the fact that there were several other places where Dodge sometimes bedded down for the night. This was his favourite haunt. Zak was sure he'd turn up here at some point tonight. "We could find a caff," he suggested. "Have something to eat then come back later."

Zak's stomach growled. He hadn't eaten since breakfast.

Rina moved a couple of paces away from Zak, turning her back and taking the Mob out of her pocket, tapping rapidly on its screen with two fingers.

She'd done that just before they'd left the empty shop – crossing the room and tapping at the screen, angling the Mob so he couldn't see what she was doing. But he guessed that secret agents were taught to keep stuff to themselves.

He pushed his hands into his pockets and walked to

the end of the archway. It was odd, he suddenly realized. Somewhere along the line he'd started to really believe she was a secret agent.

He thought back a few hours – back to the games arcade. He'd been playing Ice Thunder – on the Super-Advanced track, with seven power-ups under his belt and three nuke-snowballs in his arsenal. Highest score ever.

Then Spizz had come barrelling into him and his world had turned upside down. And here he was now – on the run with a teenage spy!

Incredible.

He heard the sound of the van before he saw it. A low, dangerous growl. Like a tiger prowling in the twilight.

Almost without thinking, he stepped into shadow as the black transit van nosed along the narrow street. The headlights were off and the cab was in darkness.

Zak's heart crashed against his ribs. His stomach tightened.

No. It couldn't be them. No way.

How . . . ?

The van came to a halt. The driver's door opened and a light flashed on in the cab. Zak saw Blondie – and another guy with a shaved head.

He stumbled backwards, then turned and ran along the archway.

"It's them!" he gasped, grabbing at Rina's arm. "They've found us."

She snatched at his wrist. "Don't panic," she said, her eyes gleaming. "It's fine."

"No! It isn't!" said Zak, tugging at her. "It's Blondie – the blond guy with the knife. I saw him. They'll kill us. We have to get out of here."

He sprinted to the far end of the archway. A walkway ran alongside a high wall. At the end it came into the loading bay of the railway station – and from there they could make for the main road. There would be plenty of people. They'd be safe.

He glanced back. Rina was still staring across the flaming bin towards the wide gape of the arch. What was she doing? Was she going to try and fight those guys?

He hesitated. Should he go back and help her?

Are you out of your tiny mind?

No . . . but . . .

Then Rina turned and ran. "You're right," she said. "Let's go."

Running wasn't really an option when they hit the main road. There were too many people moving up and down the pavements – and too much solid traffic for them to cross easily to the other side.

They moved quickly, zigzagging between pedestrians, worming through bunches of people standing outside shops and restaurants. The lights were coming on all over. In the distance Zak could see the high silvery arc of the London Eye against the darkening sky, the slowly revolving pods lit up like beacons.

He glanced over his shoulder into a sea of moving faces.

Had they lost the two men?

He caught a glimpse of a shark-eyed face under blond hair. Their eyes met for a moment.

Gotcha!

Blondie barged through the crowds, pushing people aside. He moved in a lopsided way, still favouring his injured leg.

The other man was there, too – the man with the shaved head. Zak saw him dart off the pavement, running along the gutter where he could move more quickly, traffic grazing past him as he went.

Zak stared at Rina, hoping she'd know what to do.

She nodded – she'd seen the men. She took his hand and they sped through the crowds, Rina knifing her way between people, creating a path for Zak to follow.

But the guy with the shaved head was almost with

them now – and Blondie wasn't far behind, despite his crocked knee and the indignant shouts of the people he was knocking out of the way.

"In here!" hissed Rina, snaking off to the left. "Follow my lead."

They shoved past a crowd of people queuing to get into a cinema. A guy in a blue shirt stepped in front of them.

"Hey! Wait your turn!"

"My friend's sick – we just need the toilet!" said Rina.

"No way!" The man widened his arms as she tried to dive past.

"You want him to throw up right here?" Rina exclaimed.

Zak pulled a pained face, one hand coming up over his mouth. He made retching noises and jerked his shoulders up and down as though he was about to unload his dinner over the guy's shiny black shoes.

The guy grimaced and stepped aside, pointing across the busy lobby. "That way – get him out of here!"

The sign for the toilets took them along a corridor out of sight of the lobby. As soon as they turned the corner, Rina let go of Zak's hand.

"You catch on fast," she said. "Now we need to find a back way out."

There was a short flight of steps down to closed double doors. Screen D.

Zak could hear a lot of amplified noise from beyond the doors. A movie was playing. They slipped into the darkened auditorium.

There was mayhem on the big screen. Zak could see that something was going on in a nightclub – a fight of some sort with a soundtrack of hammering bass-heavy music that made the floor throb under his feet.

Rina dipped her hand into her backpack and took out what looked like a pair of tinted glasses. She put her mouth close to Zak's ear so he could hear her above the noise of the soundtrack. "Use these – they'll help."

Puzzled, he put the glasses on. The change was startling. The dark had turned into a hundred bright shades of green. He could see everything – the rows of seats in front of them, the heads and shoulders of the people watching the movie.

The huge screen itself was a dazzling blaze of eye-wateringly white light; so bright that Zak couldn't look at it without being blinded.

"What about you?" he yelled in her ear.

"Trained," she replied. "Better in the dark than you." She pointed across the packed auditorium. "You go first. Make for the exit sign."

The sign was a bright green blaze to one side of the howling screen. He nodded.

He made his way across the back of the auditorium. Ear-splitting automatic weapon fire shook the walls. Some kind of gun battle had broken out in the nightclub up on the screen – it sounded as though a world war was going on – and the music just kept battering away behind the amplified screaming and shouting.

Rina's fingers dug warningly into his arm. He glanced back. A wedge of bright green showed where the doors to the auditorium had been opened. Two shapes slid in and the door swung closed. Zak could see the two men quite clearly – and even though they looked weird and spooky in shades of night-vision green, he recognized Blondie and the bald guy.

He brought his mouth to Rina's ear. "It's them." He couldn't believe how easily the two men had found them! Did they have heat-seeking radar or something?

She made a downwards motion with her hand and they both dropped to a crouch against the wall. She pointed to the long slope of carpet that led to the exit sign. They crept along, keeping their heads down.

Then Zak spotted a point of brilliant white light roaming the walls – like a tiny spotlight. He lowered his glasses for a moment to try and figure out what it was. The light was red now – no bigger than a five pence piece – gliding to and fro across the walls.

"Night scope," Rina hissed in his ear. "Laser sights. That means a gun – probably with a silencer."

Zak's stomach lurched. He lifted his head, sliding the glasses over his eyes again and peering back between the oblivious audience munching their popcorn and sucking at their soft drinks. Blondie had a handgun – the beam of red light was coming from it.

He saw the shaved guy thump Blondie's shoulder and point – straight at him.

Zak ducked – too late. He'd been seen! The burning point of light streaked across the auditorium. Zak didn't hear the gun go off – either Rina was right and it had a silencer, or the noise on-screen blotted it out – but he heard a crack as a bullet hit the wall just above his head. It left a small, neat hole. He had never even seen a gun in real life before today – and the thought of someone shooting at him was absolutely terrifying.

Rina tugged his sleeve. "Wait for me," she mouthed. "Keep down." Like he needed telling! He watched as she crept down to the exit sign. He saw the door open and close quickly. Then she came creeping back.

Clever. Blondie and his mate would think they'd gone out that way. Rina pointed. He nodded and crawled to an aisle, then snaked across the auditorium on his belly with Rina behind him. Some people stared down as he slunk past their feet, but no one seemed to care much – they probably thought it was just a couple of kids messing about.

Playing at spies.

He didn't dare raise his head again – if Blondie had a beam on him, he might get the next bullet between his eyes.

When he finally dared a quick look, he saw two green shapes gliding along the far wall – moving towards the exit sign.

Rina's mouth was against his ear again. "Double back," she said.

He slithered to the back of the auditorium. He got to his knees, craning his neck. He saw the exit door open and the two green figures slink through. It had worked!

Gripping Rina's hand, he got to his feet and they ran for the doors they had come in through.

Rina dragged him across the corridor and into the women's toilets. She slammed the door behind them, reaching quickly into her backpack and pulling out something small. She stooped and slipped it under the door. Blinded by the bright lights in there, Zak took off the night-vision glasses. He saw that the thing was a metal wedge.

She looked at him. "Close," she breathed. "Too close."

His ears were ringing from the noise of the movie. "They shot at us," he gasped, still not quite believing it. "But it was so loud in there no one heard it."

"I know," said Rina. She smiled and rested her hands on his shoulders. "It sounded like chucking out time at the Point Blank," she said.

He stared at her. "What?"

"It's a nightclub opposite where I've been hiding out." She shook his shoulders. "It was a joke, Zak. To lighten the mood. They took a shot – they missed. Score one for us, right?"

"If you say so." He was too shocked to feel like celebrating. "But how did they know where to find us?"

"I've been thinking the same thing," Rina said. "You've got a mobile, haven't you?" She held her hand out. "Give it to me."

He took the phone out of his pocket and handed it to her. She walked over to one of the cubicles, dropped the phone into the toilet bowl and flushed.

He gaped at her, speechless.

"They have to be tracking us somehow," she said. "My Mob has a jamming app – so they can't be following us on that. It has to be your phone."

"How?" Zak gasped.

"They have surveillance capabilities that would make your eyes pop out, Zak," she said. "Trust me – they've been following us using your phone." She went to the small smoked-glass window. It was locked. She took some thin tools from her pocket and worked on the lock.

Zak stared around him. He was in a women's toilet with a teenage spy – and his mobile had just been flushed. How much weirder could this day get?

"There we go," murmured Rina, swinging the small window open. "Come on." She hitched herself up onto the frame and slithered through. He watched as her heels vanished.

He paused for a moment, half-tempted to lock himself in a cubicle and hope the craziness would all go away. Then he took a deep breath, and headed for the window. He was halfway through when he heard the gunshot.

CHAPTER **SEVEN**

Zak tumbled head first out of the window. He crashed down into a pile of black rubbish bags in an alley. He was too scared to notice the smell right away, or the sticky gooey stuff that was oozing from the bags.

He lay panting with fear, listening hard. It was difficult to hear anything over the pounding of his own blood in his ears. He risked shifting, turning himself upright. He lifted his head, separating the bin bags with his hands.

He was at the blind end of an unlit alley. Rina was curled on the ground, face down, her legs at strange angles, one arm thrown out. She wasn't moving. A figure was walking towards her – black against the lights of the distant street.

Zak's brain raced. Rina had been shot. He was next. He was going to die here.

As the figure closed in on Rina, Zak saw it was the shaven-headed man. He tried to think. It wasn't easy, not with Rina lying there in front of him, dead or badly injured. Was there any way he could escape and get to the police?

He was fast – but was he fast enough to outrun a bullet?

No. Don't be ridiculous.

It wasn't possible.

He'd be shot in the back.

A kind of grim, desperate determination filled him. If he couldn't escape, he'd go down fighting. He might even be able to save Rina if she wasn't already dead. He shifted again, getting his legs under him. The bags creaked and rustled.

The man was standing over Rina now, but his head jerked up at the sound.

He pointed his gun towards where Zak was squatting.

"Come out of there, kid," he said. "No one's going to hurt you."

Yeah, right.

Zak stood up, the bags falling away around him. His fists were clenched, every muscle tense and straining. If he could just make it across the two metres of tarmac, maybe he could grab the gun.

"Get over here," the man said, gesturing with the weapon.

Zak sprang forwards with all the strength in his legs. That guy was going to pay for what he'd done to Rina. But the bags tangled around his ankles and he went thumping down onto his face, almost at the man's feet.

"What was that?" The man's voice was mocking. "A clip from *Jackass TV*? Get up."

Feeling like an utter loser, Zak got to his hands and knees, his whole body aching from the impact on the ground.

He was startled by a sudden move from Rina. She twisted onto her back, kicking high. Her foot cracked hard on the man's wrist. He gave a shout of pain as the gun went wheeling through the air. Then she spun on her back, her outstretched foot sweeping the man's legs from under him.

She threw herself at him as he tumbled to the ground. Her arm rose and fell sharply, her hand flat like the edge of a scythe. There was a thud. The man sprawled. Out for the count.

Rina turned towards Zak, her eyes burning.

"I thought he'd shot you," Zak gasped.

"So did he," Rina said, bounding to her feet. "Quick, the other one will be coming for us," she said. "Are you good with heights?"

"Fairly," said Zak. "Why?"

She pointed. A metal ladder was stapled to the back wall of the cinema building. It stretched up to a flat roof.

She looked at him. He nodded.

"Good man," she said. "Stay close – don't look down."

She went up the ladder very fast, but Zak kept right behind her. As he was about to clamber onto the roof, he glanced down. He saw a swift-moving shape run down the alley. Limping. Blondie. He crouched by the shaven-headed man for a moment then stood, his head turning from side to side. Zak saw a square of bluish light in Blondie's hand. A mobile phone screen. He held the phone to his ear, obviously talking to someone.

Zak smiled to himself.

You don't catch us that easily, he thought.

Blondie looked up suddenly as though he'd heard Zak's thoughts. Zak's heart skipped a beat as the man ran for the ladder.

Zak flung himself onto the roof. "He's seen us," he gasped. "I'm sorry."

He was a fool. If he hadn't paused to look down, Blondie might never have figured it out.

"Don't be sorry, be smart," Rina said. She ran across the roof, the backpack bumping on her shoulders. There was a raised block with a metal door. There was no handle on the outside and it was locked.

"I should have brought some chewing gum," Rina muttered to herself, kicking the door.

Zak stared. "Some what?"

"Chewing gum," she said irritably. "C4. Plastic explosives. I could have blown the door." She shook her head. "How are you with long jumping?"

She was staring across to an adjoining rooftop.

A slow grin spread itself across Zak's face.

"You'd be surprised," he said.

Zak was feeling good about himself.

He was taking the lead now as they ran alongside a raised stretch of sloping skylights. The rooftop of the cinema was several buildings away. If Blondie *had* managed to keep on their trail, he wasn't close enough behind to be seen. Zak guessed that his injured knee would have prevented him from attempting the jumps from roof to roof.

"Okay, that was really something," Rina said. "Have you been training for the Olympics or what?"

"I'm good at running," Zak replied. "It was in my file, remember? Jumping is just running but with longer gaps between strides." He grinned. "More or less."

"Yes – but . . ." She laughed. "That last jump must have been over four metres. I probably wouldn't even have risked it – but you just went sailing over like a bird."

"You managed it all right," Zak said, pride swelling in his chest.

"By the skin of my teeth!" Rina said. "My heart's still thumping – but you acted like it was nothing."

"Oh . . . you know . . ."

Now that they had put distance between them and the thugs, they were hunting for a way back down to street level.

But then what?

"Where should we go now?" Zak asked Rina. "They know about under the arches – we can't go back there."

"Do you have any idea where Dodge will be?" Rina asked.

"Somewhere in Soho, probably," Zak replied. "Working the tourists or hunting for food around the back of restaurants." He looked at her. "He likes Chinese food – we could start with Chinese restaurants."

She lifted an eyebrow. "Chinese restaurants in Soho?" she said. "Great. That should cut it down to about twenty zillion!"

"I don't know what else to suggest," he said helplessly. "You're the secret agent – why don't *you* think of something?"

She smiled. "It's okay, Zak – you're doing fine." She took a breath, then frowned. "We need to get north of the river," she said. "Normally I'd take one of the rat runs . . . but I don't think I'd get access now my codes have been wiped."

"What are rat runs?" Zak asked.

"Secret tunnels under the Thames," she replied. "Not many people know about them. Project 17 has access, but they're protected by sec-codes."

Secret tunnels under London? Was the weirdness never going to end?

"We could just catch the tube," Zak suggested. "Or even a bus."

A grin curled her mouth. "Yes, we could," she said. "Lose ourselves in the crowd. Hide in plain sight. That might work."

The rhythmic pulse of a helicopter beat down from out of the sky. Faint, but growing louder. Rina turned slowly, her eyes searching.

"It might just be police traffic control," Zak said. "They're always hanging around."

"Maybe," Rina murmured. "Or maybe not."

She dropped to one knee, swinging the backpack around and opening it. She brought out something that looked like a thin silvery torch. She pressed a button towards one end and held it to her eye.

She swore softly under her breath.

"What is it?" Zak asked.

"Trouble," murmured Rina. "They're bringing the big guns out tonight, Zak. We're going to have to outsmart them." She ran to the edge of the roof, gripping the low parapet and leaning out to stare down into the street.

He listened to the roar of the approaching helicopter. It was a still a fair way off – like a black dragonfly against the sky. But it was definitely heading their way.

He remembered Blondie on the phone in the alley. Calling for back up.

"If they have choppers, they'll have ground troops as well," Rina said, almost as if she was talking to herself. "What would that mean? Ten Sweeper Teams? Maybe more if they can assemble them in time. Eyes on all tube stations. CCTV being relayed back to Fortress." She swore again. Zak was quite impressed by her swearing.

The helicopter was getting closer. A spotlight blazed out, like a white finger probing downwards. The beam of light flickered across the rooftops – moving towards them with deadly purpose.

Rina drew the zipper out of her backpack. Zak watched as she clamped it to the outer edge of the parapet, adjusting metal braces and tightening them to grip the brickwork.

She reeled out a few metres of the fine cabling and stretched the webbing belt between her hands. "Put the backpack on," she told him. "Ever done any abseiling?"

"No," Zak said uneasily as he secured the straps of the backpack over his shoulders.

"Don't sweat it," she said. "It's as easy as falling off a log."

Or a roof.

Budda-budda-budda-budda.

The helicopter was only two buildings away now, hovering in the night sky like some kind of prehistoric insect. The searchlight beam cut through the air. It was sneaking up on them far too quickly. It would be a matter of seconds now.

"Lift your arms and trust me." Rina's voice was urgent as she turned away from him. Zak did as he was told.

Rina pressed her back up against him, drawing the belt around them both and securing the catch, pulling it tight so he was pushed even harder against her.

She edged to the parapet of the roof — he had no choice but to shuffle along with her. His nose was in her ponytail. Her shoulder blades were digging into him. He couldn't decide whether it was the embarrassment or the discomfort of this strange situation that bothered him the most.

"Ready?" she asked.

"No," he croaked, hardly able to breathe. "Not really."

"You'll be fine." They stepped up together onto the narrow stone parapet. The spotlight beam raked across the roof towards them.

Then Rina gave a little sideways hop, and Zak went with her.

The zipper cable spooled out with an angry whirring noise as they plunged down the face of the building. Rina twisted around so she was facing the wall, kicking off every couple of metres to prevent them from smashing into the passing brickwork.

Zak hung against her back, his face in her hair, the belt almost cutting him in two. His legs paddled uselessly in the air, his arms wrapping automatically around her as the building whizzed by.

No-o-o-o-o-oooo . . .

The belt gouged deep into Zak's back and sides as the zipper suddenly slowed down, squeezing the last few bubbles of breath out of his lungs. They hit the pavement with no more impact than if they had jumped out of a ground floor window.

Rina released the belt and grabbed his hand. As they ran along, he was vaguely aware of people applauding and of puzzled and smiling faces as they sped past. Passers-by must have thought they'd been performing some kind of stunt.

"They'll see the zipper, they'll know what happened," Rina panted as they ran. "We have to get away from here. We can't trust public transport. There will be agents everywhere now. They'll be watching the bridges and all the main roads. We have to find somewhere out of range of the closed-circuit cameras."

"They can't follow us everywhere with those things," Zak said.

She glanced at him. "Are you kidding? There are over half a million CCTV cameras in London, Zak. They're everywhere. They're probably watching us right now."

For the second time that day Zak has the unpleasant sensation of crosswires on his back.

Rina darted down a side street. It was still crowded,

but it was darker here and there were fewer people and cars. Another turn and they were almost alone.

"How are we going to get across the river without being seen?" muttered Rina as they jogged along side by side.

Zak had already been giving that problem some thought.

"I have a really stupid idea," he said. "Stupid and dangerous."

"I like the sound of it so far," Rina said with a quick grin.

"Are there CCTV cameras on the railway bridges over the Thames?" he asked.

Stupid. Stupid. Stupid.

And even more dangerous than he'd imagined.

In fact, all things being equal – stupid and dangerous with great big clanging bells on.

Zak perched on the steel girder, clinging on for his life and staring down at the iron-grey waters of the River Thames, racing along some fifteen metres below him in the darkness.

Next time, he'd know to keep his big mouth shut.

The river churned and foamed as it broke around the stone pillars of the bridge, whispering and muttering to him, tempting him to let go: *Come on in, the water's lovely!*

"I told you not to look down!" Rina's voice broke him out of the trance. She was ahead of him, bent under the low cross girders, shuffling along on the narrow lip of steel, her long arms gripping the metal edges above her head as she swung herself along like a monkey through the jungle.

"I wasn't!" Zak lied, dragging his gaze away from the water. He was having trouble concentrating. It was the middle of the night. He'd had a rough day and he hadn't eaten anything for almost sixteen hours. Rina was a spy – she was used to this kind of thing. He was just an ordinary kid. He shouldn't be doing this crazy stuff.

"Hold on," Rina warned. "We have incoming!" Zak felt the steel begin to vibrate around him. Another train was coming. The roaring and rattling grew to a deafening crescendo above them, shaking the bridge, threatening to jog them from their precarious perches. Zak winced as he looked up at the huge black monster with its screaming and screeching wheels.

The noise filled his head, shaking his bones. He felt his fingers slipping. He twisted, turning his face to the girder, gritting his teeth, trying to snatch a stronger grip with his numbed fingers.

He would fall. He knew he would.

He felt a firm hand in the small of his back, holding him steady.

The train thundered overhead. It would never end. But then it was gone and the noise and the vibrations began to subside.

Zak gasped for breath. He could taste blood in his mouth. He must have bitten his lip.

"Are you okay?" Rina's voice was close. He opened his eyes and turned to look at her.

He was about to make a comment about people who ask stupid questions when something happened. He heard a sharp whining sound and felt a burning sensation on his cheek. At exactly the same moment – so it seemed – he heard the hard crack of metal on metal and he saw Rina jerk her head back.

Her feet slipped and she fell. Zak's reaction was instinctive – he had no time to think. Clinging on with one hand, he lunged for her and caught her arm just above the elbow as she dropped. It felt as if his arm was being pulled out at his shoulder, and his fingers were slipping on the metal lip above his head.

For a moment, Rina hung there as a dead weight, but then she snatched at the rail, hooked a knee up over the rim of the girder and hoisted herself back onto the narrow lip of black metal.

Gasping, Zak let go as she got carefully to her feet. They looked at one another and, for a moment, he thought he saw something like respect in her eyes.

Rina nodded towards a small silver-grey indentation in the black steel – at head height, only a fraction from where she had been standing. Raw and fresh.

"A bullet did that," she hissed. "There's a sniper. They've found us." She looked into his alarmed face. "This isn't going to work, Zak. Are you a strong swimmer?"

His throat tightened in fear. "Yes."

"If you get into difficulties in the water, just hang on to me," she told him as she grabbed his hand, stepped into empty air, and pulled him after her.

The dark water was waiting to swallow them. It was as black as oil under the bridge. Seething. Malicious. Terrifying.

He closed his eyes, feeling his clothes snapping as he fell. He heard the wind rushing past his ears. He felt Rina's fingers like a vice around his hand.

Then he hit the water. The sudden cold cut him like a knife. He had forgotten to take a deep breath. The icy water closed over his head. He kicked wildly in the freezing blackness. Rina's hand slipped away.

He plunged downwards.

Alone now.

The deep dark water was laughing in his ears.

Telling him that he was going to drown.

CHAPTER **EIGHT**

It was a small square room without windows. An array of eight plasma screens filled the wall above a desk crammed with electronic equipment: scanners and printers and wireless keyboards, hubs and switchers and GPS receivers. Against the wall were rows of computer towers and modules and other, less obvious devices with blinking lights and blue phase mode LCD displays. Cables trailed across the desk and hung down in tangles onto the floor.

A boy sat in an executive office armchair, his knees drawn up and his feet on the edge of the desk as he typed rapidly on a keyboard that rested across his thighs. He was about twelve years old, small and thin with a round face and light brown hair combed down into a deep fringe that almost hid his slightly bulging black eyes.

There were posters and cards and cut-out pictures pinned and taped to the other walls. Pictures of frogs. Lots of different frogs. And sitting in among all the computer equipment were a whole lot more frogs – plastic frogs, wind-up clockwork frogs, plush frogs, frog beanbags, frogs made from shells, playing musical instruments. Frogs from all over.

The boy was really into frogs.

As he typed with swift, pecking fingers, his eyes darted from screen to screen. On each screen, there was a different scene. Night scenes. Live-feed CCTV scenes of London streets.

A disembodied man's voice cut through the tapping of the keyboard and the hum of electronics.

"How's it going, Bug?"

The boy called Bug frowned, as though irritated by the interruption. "Fine, Control."

"Do you have all the pieces?" asked the voice.

Bug's eyes flickered over the screens. "Pretty much," he said, his voice clipped and oddly businesslike for a twelve year old. "They've gone dark for the moment – under Hungerford Bridge. I'll pick 'em up on the other side. But there's something strange about Archer, Control. Something you'd be interested in."

"Strange?" The man sounded intrigued.

"Yes. He's quick," Bug replied. "I mean very quick. Quicker than I've ever seen. I'll patch you over some footage from the helicopter and CCTV. He's way faster than Rina. In the dash to the railway bridge, he had to keep stopping for her to catch up." His fingers danced over the keyboard. "And he jumps like . . ." A smile curled his lips. ". . . Like an Amazonian rocket frog!"

"Interesting," said the man's voice. "What about Barracuda? What's the latest?"

"No change, Control," Bug replied. "Latest intel I have is that Barracuda is due in London tomorrow."

"Excellent," said the man. "Keep me in the loop."

"I will."

There was a click as the connection cut. The boy called Bug went back to scanning the plasma screens with his slightly odd, staring eyes, while his fingers tapped at the keyboard and the surveillance pictures continued to change.

*

Zak floundered in the blind water, kicking wildly, clawing upwards with his arms. His chest was painful from the lack of air and the water sang in his ears. It was hard to think.

So cold!

The ache swelled under his ribs until he couldn't fight it any more. He took a breath – and his lungs filled with air. He coughed, sinking again, swallowing water. But now his brain was working. He pushed up to the surface, treading water, swirling his arms around him to keep buoyant, like he'd learned in school.

He took a moment to wipe his hair out of his eyes. A dazzle of lights streaked across his blurred vision. The far bank of the river. Looping strings of pinpoint lights along the embankment. Lit-up buildings facing the Thames. Towers of square lights where skyscrapers jutted up into the night sky. All the bright lights of London.

"Rina!" His voice sounded weak and faint in his ears. The flow of the river had pulled him out from under the deep shadow of the bridge. He turned slowly, scanning the choppy surface of the river – trying to make out her bobbing head in the confusion of dark and light ripples.

"Rina!"

The banks seemed so far away. The water was so cold. A huge, black shape came churning towards him, pushing a whitish wake ahead of its blunt prow.

A river barge.

Zak swam desperately for the near shore. The black shape loomed over him. He was lifted in the swell, then dropped again into a trough of black water. He coughed, his mouth filling with foam as the barge barrelled past him.

He fought against the suction as the barge ploughed on, doing his best to keep his head up as the wake churned and boiled around him.

He got to the bank, exhausted and desperate. But there was nothing to cling to – and no way up the slimy green wall of the river. He clawed at the brickwork, leaving long streaks in the foul-smelling algae.

No! It was hopeless. He needed to find somewhere to climb out – before he was too weak to keep above the water.

He heard a chugga-chugga noise, getting louder. A cone of blue-white light slithered over the choppy water. He heard a voice. A curved, dark-blue shape filled his vision. The hull of a tall boat. Large white letters danced in his eyes.

POLICE

A black pole reached down towards him. There was a wide hook on the end. He snatched at it with both hands and clung on with all his remaining strength.

Zak sat on a low bench in a police cell. He had a blanket over his shoulders and he was ravenously eating a burger and fries from a plastic tray. He was warm and dry and for the first time since Spizz had crashed down dead at his feet, he felt safe.

His rescue from the river was a blur. He had been fished out by the Marine Police and swaddled in a silvery thermal body wrap while they sped to a landing point. A police car had been waiting and he'd been brought to this police station – he wasn't sure where it was, and he didn't really care. A friendly officer had got him to strip off his wet things and had given him a tracksuit top and bottoms five times too big for him, as well as a large blanket.

They'd asked him a few questions to find out who he was and where he lived, then they'd put him in the cell and given him something to eat. They'd left the door open, but told him to stay put and yell if he needed anything. They hadn't mentioned scooping a girl out of the river, and he didn't think Rina would want him talking about her. *I was with a teenage spy, actually, she was on the run.* No, that wouldn't have been a good idea. But he did wonder where she was right now. Had she got out of the river safely? Was she worried about him?

He was just finishing the food when a woman police officer came into the cell, carrying his clothes. "There you are, Zak," she said, smiling. "Still warm from the launderette drier. Feeling more with it now?"

Zak nodded. "Yes, thanks," he said. "Are Paul or Kath on their way?"

"I think so," she said. She looked over her shoulder towards the open door. "We're a bit busy up there. Can I leave you to it? Do you need anything else?"

Two more burgers and another bucket of fries, he thought, but he shook his head. "No, thanks. I'm fine."

"Good for you." And with that, she was gone. He listened to her heels clicking on the lino for a few moments, then he got up, shed the cumbersome tracksuit and pulled on his own clothes.

He sat down again, tying his shoes.

It was over. Already it felt as if he must have dreamed the whole thing. Who would believe him if he told them? He sighed – and what would Kath and Paul have to say about him losing his mobile phone?

This mental spy girl flushed it down the toilet — honest!

He smiled to himself. He was well out of Rina's crazy world. He just hoped she'd leave him alone from now on. The girl really was totally off her head!

Then he remembered Spizz's dead eyes and the smile faded.

He heard footsteps approaching. One set. Paul?

But it wasn't one of the social workers that came to the open doorway and looked in at him. It was a tall grey-haired man in a very expensive suit. He had a lean, rugged face and steely grey eyes, and he was carrying a steaming mug in one hand.

The man smiled and stepped into the cell. "So, Zak, how are you doing?"

"Fine, thanks," Zak said as the man sat at his side, very stiff and straight. He offered the mug and Zak saw that it was hot chocolate.

Zak had the curious feeling that he'd seen this man before. But when and where?

"Do you mind if I ask you a few questions?" the man said amiably.

Zak sipped the thick chocolate drink. "No. Ask away."

"How did you wind up in the Thames, Zak? What happened?"

Zak was about to tell him the whole bizarre tale when an image flashed into his mind. The image of a tall, grey-haired man standing on the steps of Robert Wyatt House, talking to Paul.

Zak gulped the chocolate and had a coughing fit. The man took the mug from him and patted him on the back as he choked and gurgled.

"Steady there," he said. "Did it go down the wrong way?"

Zak nodded, his eyes watering.

By the time he had recovered, he was almost certain that this was the same guy he'd seen through the snakescope. One of the team that Rina had told him was the enemy.

He sipped carefully at the steaming chocolate, on the alert now – wondering what on earth to do.

"So – your little swim?" the man asked again.

"I fell in," Zak said.

"And how did you come to do that, Zak?"

"Oh, you know," Zak said guardedly. "The usual way."

The man gazed at him levelly, but there was nothing in his expression to give Zak the least idea of what he was thinking. "What about the girl?" he asked. "Do you know where we could find her?"

Zak blinked at him. "What girl?" He didn't necessarily

trust Rina, but he wasn't about to give up a load of information about her to some strange guy in a police station.

A cold smile stretched across the man's face. "Did you believe her, Zak?" he asked. "Did you really fall for all that stuff she told you?" He shook his head. "You look like a smart kind, Zak. Did any of it sound likely?"

He looked into the man's eyes. There was a long silence. Zak wished the man would say something to break the tension.

"Paul should be here soon," Zak said, his nose in the mug. "Then I can go home." He looked at the man. "Can't I? It's not like I'm under arrest or anything."

The man pushed his hand into his jacket pocket. His fist came out clenched around something. He moved so suddenly and so quickly that Zak didn't have time to react. One hand grabbed Zak's hair and jerked his head sideways while the clenched fist came up to his throat. Zak felt a sharp stinging sensation.

The half-full mug went crashing to the floor, exploding in pieces and sending the hot chocolate spraying everywhere. The man held Zak against the wall with one hand to his chest.

Zak was about to struggle when he suddenly felt very odd.

"Don't fight it, Zak," he heard the man say. "Just let go."

Zak felt as though he was floating in a grey cloud. He was vaguely aware of being picked up and carried along a tiled corridor. Up a flight of stairs. Out through a door and into a dark street. There was a black transit van waiting at the kerb. The walls wheeled around his head and the night sky opened and closed like yawning mouths.

He was bundled into the back of the van. He heard the man's voice speaking. "I've got him." There was a pause as if he was listening to a voice Zak couldn't hear. "No, she wasn't with him. I'm on my way. Expect me in ten."

The door slammed shut and he was in dreamy, floating darkness, lying staring up at a metal roof.

He heard a door clang and an engine start up. The floor began to vibrate underneath him. Odd, coloured lights revolved in the air above. He watched them with blank eyes, quite liking them, lifting his arms to try and grab at them, but not minding that they always drifted out of reach before he could close his fingers on them.

Rina's voice echoed softly in his woolly mind.

If those guys find us, we're both dead meat, do you get that?

Dead meat.

Oh – that was bad. Wasn't it? Very *bad*! He should do something. He struggled to sit up but his body felt too heavy. The coloured lights whirled around him and he slumped back into silence.

CHAPTER **NINE**

When Zak woke up he was in a strange room. Lying on a cold lino floor, he stared up at a ceiling crossed by massive riveted steel girders painted red. Woozy and with rubbery legs, he got slowly to his feet.

There were no windows. Maps covered most of the space on the walls – faded maps marked out with curved lines of little pins. There were wooden desks. Steel-framed chairs. Filing cabinets. A row of old fashioned telephones that wouldn't have looked out of place in a museum.

There was a smell – musty. Old paper. Stale air. There

were cobwebs everywhere, hanging between the telephones, forming dusty hammocks across the ceiling. Nesting in corners.

Trying to make sense of it all, Zak walked unsteadily over to one of the maps. It showed Europe and the United Kingdom. The pins ran in double lines across France. He looked closer, intrigued and puzzled. Some of the pins had little Nazi swastikas attached.

"World War II," he murmured to himself. "The invasion of Europe. D-Day!" Paul and Kath encouraged the kids to watch the History Channel. Zak knew a bit about the Second World War.

He walked around, checking out the other maps on the walls. They were all from the same period. The 1940s. Following the progress of the war.

So weird.

Where was he?

He was feeling more with it now. He walked towards the door. It was locked. He pressed his ear to the panels. Listening.

Nothing.

He hammered on the door. "Hey! Let me out! You can't do this! Hey!" He tried kicking the door, but still no one came in response to the noise.

"What have you brought me here for?" he shouted.

The silence was unnerving. "This is kidnapping, I hope you realize that! You're going to be in so much trouble if you don't let me out right now." He thumped hard on the door with the heels of both hands. "Hey!"

He glared at the locked door then walked over to one of the chairs and sat down heavily, his elbows on his knees and chin in his hands.

What would Rina have done? Well, for a start, she'd have had that nifty backpack full of gadgets to call on. He imagined himself taking the little metal tools out of his own pocket as she'd done in the cinema toilets to unlock the window. He'd pick the lock and be out of there in no time.

He gazed up at the bare light bulb. At least they hadn't left him in the dark. He wondered what time it was. The early hours of the morning, he guessed. Paul or Kath or someone must have got to the police station by now. They'd be asking questions. Worried about him.

He looked at the door. Any minute now, it would be unlocked and Paul would march in with his permanently anxious expression and Zak would be taken home. He could hear Paul's voice in his head.

What did you get yourself into this time, Zak?

He heard the click of a key. The door swung open and the grey-haired man stepped in, carrying a tray.

"Are you feeling any ill effects, Zak?" he asked.

"I want to go home," Zak said. He knew he should be afraid, but he was more angry and worn out than fearful.

"All in good time," said the man.

Zak got up, pushing the chair away, his voice so loud that it surprised him. "No!" he shouted. "Now!"

The man put the tray on a desk and drew himself a chair. He sat down, crossing his legs and leaning back, looking calmly at Zak, his elbows on the arms of the chair and his fingertips steepled together.

"We're thirty metres below street level, Zak," he said. "Shouting isn't going to get you anywhere." He gestured to the tray. There were various cans of soft drinks along with chocolate bars and packets of crisps. "Help yourself if you're hungry."

Zak stood behind his chair, glaring at the man. He didn't want food. He just wanted out.

"My name is Colonel Hunter," said the man. "And I can assure you that you are in absolutely no danger."

"That's not what I've been told," Zak said. He narrowed his eyes, remembering that Rina had mentioned a Colonel Hunter. "If you're in charge of Project 17, you're an idiot for believing Switchblade over Rina. He's a liar!"

Colonel Hunter's face remained impassive. "Project

17?" he said. "I've never heard of it, Zak. What is it?"

Zak seethed with anger. "One of your Sweeper Teams killed my friend," he spat. "And they shot at me."

"What's a Sweeper Team, Zak?" Colonel Hunter asked.

Oh – so that's how he was going to play it . . .

Zak took a few long, deep breaths to calm himself. Colonel Hunter was as cold as ice. Yelling wasn't going to get him anywhere. He needed to try and psych this guy out. Cool for cool.

He moved from behind the chair and sat down. He grabbed a chocolate bar and peeled open the wrapper. He leaned back, crossing his legs just like Colonel Hunter, and began to bite chunks off the chocolate.

"This is nice," he said, holding it out. "Want some?"

He hoped he sounded more confident than he felt.

Colonel Hunter smiled and shook his head.

"You remind me of someone I met some years ago," he said. "Same attitude – same stubborn streak. Same determination to beat the fear. Still, I suppose . . ." He stopped as though thinking better of what he had almost said. "I've read your files, Zak," he continued. "There's nothing in your social services file about your family."

There was a pause. "So what?" Zak responded. "I was left outside a hospital – like a parcel. They obviously weren't interested." He'd never felt sorry for himself for not having parents. He looked sharply at the Colonel. "Do you know anything about them, then?"

Colonel Hunter gazed at him for a few moments, as though considering his response. "There's nothing I can tell you about your family, Zak," he said. "I'm sorry."

"It's no big deal," Zak replied. "When are you going to let me go home?"

"Soon," said Colonel Hunter. "I need to ask you a few questions first. I need to hear your side of the story. You've been keeping some pretty unsavoury company recently, wouldn't you say?"

"Not on purpose," Zak said. "Anyway, from what I've been told, you're the scary people, not Rina."

"And am I scary, Zak?" the Colonel asked.

Zak looked at him. "I don't know – are you?"

"That depends," the Colonel said with another of his unreadable smiles. "I don't know exactly what Ballerina has been telling you, but the truth is she's a traitor to this country." He leaned forwards, his eyes hard. "You know what a traitor is, don't you, Zak?"

"Of course I do,' Zak said, feeling a little uneasy now. There was something about those cold grey eyes. "But you're wrong. She was framed."

"Is that what she told you?"

"Switchblade is the real traitor," Zak said.

"You trust Ballerina?"

Zak felt a moment of doubt. Why *should* he trust her? It was her fault he was in this mess in the first place. "I don't know," he said hesitantly. "But why should I trust you more?"

Colonel Hunter sighed and leaned back again. "Do you know where she can be found?"

"No," Zak retorted. "And I wouldn't tell you if I did. You'd just send your killers out to get her."

"They aren't my killers, Zak," said the Colonel. "I don't have people killed. I just want to stop her from handing over secrets of national importance to a foreign power." His hands gripped the metal arms of his chair. "We're the good guys, Zak."

"If you're so good, why don't you let me go home?" Zak asked. "I've told you I don't know where Rina is. A real good guy would get in touch with my social workers and have them come and pick me up."

The Colonel looked at him thoughtfully. "We've been monitoring you for the last few hours, Zak," he said. "Watching you with remote cameras. That running thing you do – and those jumps!" His eyebrows lifted. "Pretty impressive – but you know that already, don't you?"

Zak shrugged. He wasn't about to be soft-soaped into helping this man to kill Rina.

"Do you know what you want to do with your life, Zak?" the Colonel asked in a lighter voice. Deliberately changing the subject. Good cop/bad cop – all rolled into one. "You have good grades – you could probably go to any university you chose if you worked a little harder."

Zak stared at the floor. He had never liked "could-do-better" pep talks about his schoolwork.

"Some people get a real sense of fulfilment from public service," Colonel Hunter said. "You might want to think about that."

Zak looked up at him. Public service? What did that even mean?

"Thanks," he said blankly. This was all so new to him. He was still trying to figure everything out. "That's good advice. Can I go now?"

Colonel Hunter stared at him intently. "You really don't know where Rina is?" he asked.

Zak looked straight back. "I haven't a clue," he said.

The Colonel got up. "Then I don't see what else can be gained by keeping you here," he said. "I'll call the children's home – have someone come and collect you." He walked to the door and opened it. He turned. "You've had a strange day, haven't you, Zak?" he said. "Well, it's over now. Go home. Get some sleep. Forget everything you've seen and heard."

He took one of the silvery Mobs out of his jacket pocket and started tapping on it with his thumb as he walked out of the room. He closed the door firmly. Zak heard the click of a key in the lock. He jumped up and ran to the door, pressing his ear to the panels again.

Colonel Hunter's voice was muffled but quite clear. "No, he won't play along," he heard the Colonel say. "I know. Big shame." A pause. "No. He knows too much for that to be a safe option." Another gap, then: "I've told him he'll be picked up. Can you get a Sweeper Team here in ten minutes? Okay. Green-light that. Pity – I liked him."

The voice continued, but Colonel Hunter was moving away from the room now, and Zak couldn't hear anything else that was said.

He didn't need to. He leaned against the door, his body shivering with icy chills, a weight like a ball of lead in the pit of his stomach.

The Colonel had just arranged to have him killed.

He backed away from the door and was brought up sharp by the edge of the chair hitting him behind the knees. He sat down, sucking in air, trying to think. The door was locked. It opened inwards, so there was no way to barge it open.

He got up and walked around the room, not sure what he was looking for, hoping for some kind of inspiration. Heart thumping. A bitter taste in his mouth. Trying not to panic.

He paused, staring at the wall above one of the filing cabinets. There was some kind of vent there, covered by a metal grille. If he could shift the grille – would the hole behind be large enough to slither through?

It had to be worth a try. He searched the desks, finding a letter opener to use as a tool. He went back to the filing cabinet. He flexed his legs and jumped, snatching hold of the top of the cabinet and scrambling up onto it. Hunched under the ceiling, he jabbed at the screws holding the grille to the wall. He had to scrape old paint off the heads, but once he got the edge of the letter opener into the groove, he found the screws turned relatively easily. He was hot now. Sweat rolled down his face.

Only one screw left. He had a sudden inspiration. He loosened the screw a little then swung the grille to reveal the vent. Cold air wafted over him. The vent was thick with dirt and cobwebs.

Turning himself around awkwardly, he lifted his feet

into the vent and pushed off with his hands, sliding backwards into the darkness. Once he was cocooned in the vent, he twisted the grille back into place and slipped the letter opener through to hold it level.

He hoped that from a distance, no one would notice the screws were missing. That might give him a few extra minutes to get out of here.

He squirmed backwards along the metal duct. The banded square of light from the room shrank. His feet clanged on metal. He tried to work out what to do next.

Then he let out a gasp of relief. His feet had hit against another vent. There was a dim light beyond. A room! He kept perfectly still, listening hard. Voices? Any sound of people moving about in the room?

Nothing. He drew his knee up as far as he could in the confines of the vent and kicked out. The grille clanged but held. He kicked again – he was hot and uncomfortable and desperate.

Kick! Kick!

Finally he felt something give. He boosted himself backwards, pushing the grille away with his feet. He felt empty air under his legs. A final couple of pushes and he dropped from the vent into another room.

Light was coming in through a frosted glass panel in the door. He could make out rows of small desks, each with an ancient typewriter on it. He ran to the door.

It was unlocked. He opened it a fraction onto a long dim-lit corridor.

He hesitated for a moment, then slid out into the corridor and ran.

CHAPTER **TEN**

Colonel Hunter stood behind Bug's chair in the room with the plasma screens. The images on the screens were different now. They showed rooms and corridors. One of the rooms had old maps on the walls. Maps showing the Allied invasion of Nazi-occupied Europe in 1944.

Bug tapped at his keyboard and the scene shifted and zoomed in to show a pair of hands moving a grille back into place above one of the filing cabinets.

"He's resourceful," said the Colonel. "I like the way he's covering his tracks." He leaned forwards, watching intently, resting his hands on Bug's shoulders. Bug made an irritated noise and twitched his shoulders.

Colonel Hunter lifted his hands away. "Sorry, Bug," he said.

Bug tapped the keyboard and they watched as Zak came out of the air duct in the typists' office, covered in dust and cobwebs, his face running with sweat.

The camera followed Zak to the door then lost him as he slipped into the corridor.

"Okay, Bug," said the Colonel. "Give Switchblade the green light – let's help Mr Archer on his way."

Bug was wearing a headset. He tapped his keyboard and spoke into the mike. "Game on, Switch. Operation Party Popper is go!"

"On it," came a voice.

"Now then," said Hunter as they watched Zak running along the corridor. "Let's find out what you're made of, Mr Archer."

Zak hit a T-junction in the corridor. He pressed himself against the wall, mimicking Rina's actions earlier in the day. Darting a glance around the corner, checking everything was okay before moving on. He chose the left hand turn – the corridor ran on, straight as a ruler, closed doors breaking up the smooth bare walls on either side every twenty or so paces.

Zak had realized that the corridors must be in use. The dim fluorescent tubes wouldn't be on otherwise. He came to another junction. Ve-e-ery careful. Pause. Glance. Move on. Closed doors. Steel girders across the ceiling.

What had the Colonel said? *We're thirty metres below street level, Zak.*

He needed to find some stairs – and soon – before they discovered he was missing and locked the whole place down.

He had an idea of where he was. He remembered it from a programme on the History Channel. During the Second World War, a whole subterranean city of offices and corridors had been dug out under London so the government could keep working while the bombs rained down. He must be in part of that network of underground shelters, unchanged for over seventy years.

What an incredible place!

He thought he heard something.

He stopped, twisting his head to look back the way he had come.

A voice? Muffled. In the distance.

He held his breath.

He heard running feet. He was close to another corner. He glided around it and pressed to the wall, listening.

Running footsteps for sure. Coming his way.

The voice again.

"Level four, sector C2 clear."

He knew that voice, and it surprised him to hear it.

Switchblade! The last time Zak had seen him, he'd been sprawled unconscious in an alley.

Then there was silence.

Odd. Had he gone the other way?

Zak dared a look around the corner. Switch was there – about two metres away. His blue eyes widened. Switch was wearing an earpiece.

"Target acquired!" he shouted, lunging forwards.

Rats! Stupid!

Zak turned and ran with Switchblade hard on his heels.

"What did I tell you, Control?" said Bug, switching rapidly from camera to camera as Zak went sprinting along the corridor. "He's leaving Switchblade standing."

Colonel Hunter pursed his lips as he watched the gap growing between one of his fittest agents and the boy who was racing away from him. "He makes it look effortless, too," muttered Hunter. "Is it just hard training, or is there something else going on here?"

"Like what?" asked Bug.

"I don't know. Can you patch this through to the white coats? I'd like a scientific appraisal of the boy's abilities. I think we might be onto something rather special here."

Bug followed Zak with one camera after another. They watched as he hit a pair of swing doors. A tap on the keyboard. The camera angle looked downwards at a spiral staircase of red steel. A split second later, Zak came bounding up the stairs, taking them four at a time. He looked scared but he was breathing normally and there was no sign of strain on his face.

"Look at him go!" said Bug. "If he was one of us, we could give him the codename Leapfrog."

Hunter gave a grim smile. "I think we might be able to come up with something a little better than that, if the time came," he said. "Contact Jackhammer and Wildcat – tell them to close down everything but Sector A. Let's squeeze him out of here."

Bug looked up at the Colonel. "Are you sure he'll lead us to Ballerina?" he asked, his fingers still tapping.

"I think it's fifty-fifty," said the Colonel. "Ninety-nine kids out of a hundred would just head for home – but I'm not sure about Mr Archer. I think it could go either way." He stared at the screen as Zak ran past the camera. "Come on, Zak," he said under his breath. "Don't let me down."

Zak leaned over the curving rail of the spiral staircase. Listening. He was a little out of breath now, and he could feel a stretching, tingling sensation in his thighs and calves from the effort of sprinting up those winding metal steps.

The staircase had passed three landings. He *must* be near the surface. There was no sound of pursuit.

"I suppose he could have taken a lift," he murmured under his breath. He frowned. Did they even have lifts back when this place was dug out?

He turned and nudged at a pair of swing doors.

Creak.

He paused for a moment then glided into yet another corridor. The scale of this underground world was staggering. You could house a whole army of spies down here and no one up above in the real world would know a thing about it.

Amazing.

The *real* world. Yes – that was where Zak was heading. On this level there were no rooms, he noticed. The walls were plain grey concrete.

He came to a place where his corridor intersected another one running side to side. A crossroads.

Several of the fluorescent tubes were out along the left-hand turn, and the others were flickering so the light strobed creepily. A figure stood halfway down the corridor, appearing and disappearing as the light came and went. A girl with short, spiky ash-blond hair. She was wearing white jeans and a white vest, and as the light flashed, Zak could see the sharp contours of her well-toned arm muscles.

She didn't move. She just watched him, with deep-set black eyes and a black-lipstick smile curving her mouth.

She lifted an arm and beckoned with one crooked finger. The nail was also painted black.

Zak shot a look along the other corridor.

A boy stood there. Very big. Built like a truck, with slicked-back brown hair and a wide face, high cheekbones and narrow eyes.

"End of the line, Zippy," said the boy. "Nowhere else to run."

The breath hissed between Zak's teeth.

It had been too easy.

But the boy was wrong – there was still one option. Straight ahead! Zak gathered himself and shot off across the intersection of the two corridors. The long straight run quickly allowed him to get to that special place in his mind – to that moment when the gears meshed and he could cut the air like an arrow from the bow.

He was aware of shouts and footsteps behind him – rapid, but not rapid enough. Falling behind. Scared as he was, he grinned as he ran, his legs pumping tirelessly, toes only grazing the floor, arms scything at his sides.

Yeah! How'd you like *that*? Catch me now, losers!

The end of the corridor came rushing towards him. There was a metal door.

Now what?

The door was slightly ajar. He slowed to a jog, breathing smoothly, feeling great. His mind sharp. They would never catch him. Not ever.

He yanked the door open and carried on running along a dirty unlit passageway. There was debris underfoot and the place stank. The only light filtered in from gratings above his head – but it was a few moments before he realized what that light was.

He paused, staring upwards. Street lights. And he could hear traffic now.

He came to a metal ladder that ran up to a circular metal plate in the ceiling. Glancing back, and seeing no sign of his pursuers, he climbed the ladder. The metal was cold and grimy. He hung under the hatch, pushing upwards with one hand.

No good. Too heavy. Or held down with bolts or something?

He climbed higher, pressed his back to the cold metal and heaved. There was a grating noise as the hatch lifted. Cold air blew over his face. He set his jaw and pushed harder. The hatch slid away and he sped up the ladder and out into fresh night air.

He crashed into grass, lying on his back, looking up at the cloudy London sky. Elated and relieved. Back in the real world.

Traffic rumbled close by. Buildings leaned over him. He got to his hands and knees. He was on a small patch of grass that ran alongside a high wall. Directly in front of him was a metal cabinet – a telephone substation or something. He hauled the inspection hatch back into place, letting it fall with a clang.

He stood up.

Across a wide main road filled with traffic, he saw the lit-up white stone walls of the Tower of London against the dark night sky.

His face broke into a wide smile.

He had escaped.

*

Zak was at Defcon 1. The highest possible state of alert. Ready for anything.

He hoped.

The way he saw it, he had very limited options. Colonel Hunter knew where he lived – if he went back to Robert Wyatt House, he'd be picked up again. He could call the Home, talk to Kath or Paul or whoever was on duty at this time of night – ask for help. But he had a disturbing image in his head – the image of one of the residential social workers sitting in their office, talking to him on the phone – telling him everything was fine and he could come straight back – while one of Hunter's men stood behind them with a gun to their head.

Too many movies? Maybe. Or maybe not, in the circumstances.

He couldn't go to the police – it was the cops who had handed him over to Hunter last time. He couldn't trust them.

Who could he trust?

Dodge for sure – but he didn't want to put Dodge in danger.

Rina?

Maybe – if she'd made it out of the Thames in one piece – and if he could find her. For the moment he was going to assume she was alive and that she still wanted the memory stick. He had some thoughts about how he might track her down, but first of all he wanted to try something. If he was going to ask Rina for help, then he shouldn't turn up empty-handed. Not when he could give her what she needed. What had she told him?

I just need the memory stick back – then you'll be done with me for ever.

He slid under the arches like a shadow. The oilcan fire had burned to embers. He kept to the darkest places, pressing his back to the cold brickwork, hardly daring to breathe.

He heard muted groaning and rasping snores from the sad bundles that lined the walls. He stopped, staring into the gloom, watching for any movement, for any sign that Hunter had left people here on guard.

He crept to Dodge's hardboard home and crouched at the entrance. There was silence from within. He lifted the blanket. Dodge wasn't there.

Zak sat back on his heels. Thinking hard.

Dodge must have decided to bed down on one of his other haunts. Problem was . . . which one?

Zak stood up and jogged out from under the arches. It seemed he had some more work to do tonight.

*

Zak finally tracked Dodge down to one of his hidey-holes just north of the river. The sleeping tramp was curled up in a rickety old shed in the backyard of a restaurant, protected from the elements by a ragged plastic sheet. Zak had no intention of waking him. He wasn't going to get Dodge involved. Things were hard enough for his friend without getting him mixed up in all this craziness.

He lifted the plastic sheet. He could just see Dodge's curled up legs sticking out from under other blankets. He was wearing his boots. He always slept fully clothed, huddled like an animal against the cold of night.

Dodge had draped the anorak over himself for more warmth. Zak crept closer, feeling for the pockets. Two big pockets. His fingers touched something smooth. He took hold of it and gently pulled it out and crawled away.

He looked at the wallet.

Yes!

He slipped away into the darkness. He opened the wallet and looked inside. Tucked in the change pocket was a memory stick.

The memory stick.

He closed the wallet and pushed it into the back pocket of his jeans.

Okay. Stage one completed. Now what?

He had one clue to help him track Rina down. It was something she'd said in the cinema toilets. A throwaway remark, but it had stuck in his head.

"They shot at us – but it was so loud in there no one heard it."

"I know. It sounded like chucking out time at the Point Blank."

"What?"

"It's a nightclub opposite where I've been hiding out."

He had to find the location of the Point Blank nightclub. He thought he knew the quickest way to do that.

He walked purposefully along the street. A lot of the shops and restaurants had closed down for the night. But he knew one place that stayed open 24/7. An Internet café. He'd been in there a few times but never this late.

The place was all but deserted as he pushed his way inside. A sleepy-looking teenager in a red-and-white -striped shirt was leaning on the bar, watching a small TV.

"Hot chocolate, please," Zak said. He had some money. Not much, but enough.

The teenager slouched to the back of the bar and made the hot drink.

Zak had been worried that someone might ask him what he was doing out on the streets at this time of night – but the bored teenager obviously couldn't care less.

He took the mug over to one of the side tables and perched on a stool. He opened Google on the screen and typed "Point Blank nightclub London" in the search box.

He sipped the chocolate, smiling as the search results flicked onto the screen. How easy was that?

The nightclub was in Ladbroke Grove – and there were even helpful instructions on which tube lines and bus routes to use to get there.

But he had quite a journey ahead of him – Ladbroke Grove was halfway across the city. And the tube trains wouldn't be running at this time of night.

Night buses would, though. All he needed to do was check the route.

He was just accessing the information when a heavy hand came down on his shoulder.

"What are you doing?" A man's voice.

Zak spun around.

He'd been caught!

CHAPTER **ELEVEN**

Survival instinct kicked in. Zak snatched up his half-empty mug of hot chocolate and threw the contents into the man's face, at the same moment sliding sideways off the chair and pulling away from the grabbing hand.

With a yelp of surprise, the man stumbled backwards, tripping over a chair and crashing to the floor.

Zak stared down at him. He looked old – maybe fifty or so. Just some guy. Maybe.

"Hey!" The noise seemed to have woken the teenager up. He came lurching around the counter, glaring at Zak. "What are you playing at, kid?"

The man sat up, wiping streaming chocolate off his face. "He attacked me!" he gasped, struggling to get up. "I was only going to ask him whether his parents knew where he was at this time of night – and he attacked me!"

"You shouldn't have grabbed me," exclaimed Zak, backing away towards the door. "How was I to know? You could have been anyone."

You could have been one of Hunter's Sweeper Team come to kill me.

The teenager helped the man to his feet.

The two of them stared at Zak as if he was a cornered wild animal.

"I'm okay," said the man, dabbing at his sopping coat-front with a handkerchief. "No harm done." He frowned at Zak. "A boy your age shouldn't be out and about in the middle of the night," he said. "It's not safe."

Tell me about it!

The man stepped forwards. Zak jumped back out of range. He looked harmless enough . . . but . . . ?

"Oh, for heaven's sake, boy, I'm not going to hurt you," the man said.

Zak couldn't risk it. Maybe he was paranoid – and maybe he wasn't. But he couldn't risk it. He wrenched the café door open and ran out into the night.

✻

Zak jumped off the bus. The doors unfolded and closed with a hiss and the bus rumbled away.

He huddled in his shirt and jeans, feeling the cold night air creeping over him. He was dressed for a warm summer's afternoon – not the chill of the small hours. His head was throbbing with exhaustion; he felt as if he could have just slid to the floor, curled up and slept right there in the street.

Except he couldn't. He had things to do.

The wide street was empty. A few shop fronts were illuminated, one or two upstairs windows showed a light. An occasional car cruised by.

Zak didn't know this part of London – he was trying to remember the street map from the computer screen. His brain was fuzzy with drowsiness, but he thought he knew where to go.

He walked quickly along the broad pavement, head down, hands deep in his pockets. He felt as though there were a thousand eyes on him, a thousand hands ready to snatch at him as he passed each darkened doorway. He jumped at every shadow, keeping to the kerb, ready to bolt at the slightest sign of danger.

Then he saw a neon sign up ahead. Glaring pink and blue. POINT BLANK.

He paused, slipping into cover, peering across the

street. The entrance glowed with a blue light. Two shapes stood there. Doormen, Zak assumed.

He craned his neck to see further down his side of the street. About fifty metres away, the shops ended and made way for a row of tall terraced houses set back from the road. Stone steps led up to doors hidden in porches. Lower windows were half-visible behind iron railings, dropping down below pavement level.

One of the houses was boarded up.

An empty house would make a great hiding place.

He just hoped he'd joined the dots correctly – otherwise he had no idea what to do next.

He kept close to the shopfronts, trying not to attract attention. He slid alongside the railings. One house – two – three. He was at the boarded-up house. He looked around. No one was following him. And as far as he could tell no one was watching him. He dived down the narrow stone steps to the basement flat, his heart thumping against his ribs as if it wanted to break out.

It was dark and it smelled of clogged drains. People had lobbed rubbish down here – empty beer cans and fast-food cartons. Something squished under his foot. Grimacing, he moved to the door under the main steps. The glass panels were filthy and the paint was peeling.

He pushed at the door, but it was solid. Should he

knock? Call out?

He hesitated, really wishing he had some kind of spy-craft – really wishing he knew what to do.

He glanced apprehensively over his shoulder. Jumping at nothing.

Then he noticed that the boards on the nearside of the bay window were not nailed at the bottom. He swung the boards aside, stooping to peer in through the broken window. He couldn't see much – just humped shapes in the deep gloom.

He climbed cautiously through the gap, wary of snagging himself on the remaining shards of glass that clung to the windowframe.

The boards swung closed behind him. He stood absolutely still in the room, waiting for his eyes to adjust.

A pair of those night-vision glasses would be good right now.

Slowly, the room began to reveal itself. It was a mess. There was a disgusting old sofa piled with all kinds of abandoned junk. An armchair upturned in a corner. The remains of a smashed TV set.

No sign that anyone was living here.

He picked his way across the room to the open door. There was a really unpleasant bathroom. A small kitchen. He walked along a hallway to a flight of stairs. He was about to climb them when he heard a sound from the back of the house.

Cats? Rats? He stared along the hall. There was another sound. The slow creak of a door opening. Hollow footsteps.

Not a cat, then.

He slipped around the banister and padded up a few stairs.

It might be Rina. Except that the way he remembered it, she moved silently, like a stalking leopard. Someone heavy-footed had just come into the house through the back.

It couldn't be good.

Zak bit his lip. Some of the banister's spindles were broken away. One of them was lying on the stairs. He picked it up. Just in case.

A large dark shape filled the doorway at the end of the hall. Zak caught a glimpse of blond hair.

He drew away from the banister, pressing himself against the wall, clutching the wooden spindle in both hands like a club. Terrified.

Blondie was still limping a little as he came to the end of the hallway and turned. His shark eyes flashed as he caught sight of Zak. He smiled his razor smile.

"Are you going to hit me with that thing, kid?" he asked.

"I will if you come one step closer," said Zak, annoyed that his voice was shaking so much. He felt about as menacing as a baby rabbit. Blondie would eat him alive and put the leftovers in a doggy bag for snacking on later.

"Is that a fact?" Blondie lifted one foot and brought it down on the bottom step.

Zak backed away, sliding along the wall, gripping the spindle in both fists.

Blondie lunged for him and Zak brought the spindle down hard on his groping wrist. Blondie grunted in pain, but the blow didn't stop him. His other hand went to his belt. Zak saw the dull gleam of a knife blade. And now the look on Blondie's face made his blood run cold.

He stumbled to the top of the stairs, swinging uselessly with the wooden spindle. Blondie caught hold of the end and ripped it out of Zak's hand. Zak fell backwards. The knife rose. Zak kicked out blindly.

He was lucky. His foot hit home. With a grunt, Blondie stumbled, grabbing at the banister. There was a loud crack as the banister broke away, and Blondie fell headlong over the side of the stairs, crashing heavily into the dark hallway.

Zak was panting, fighting for breath. He saw Blondie's knife glinting on the stairs. Trembling, he crept down and picked it up. Blondie was lying face down in the hallway.

Knocked out?

A long slender arm snaked past Zak's shoulder from behind. Fingers closed like a vice on his wrist. A second arm glided over his other shoulder, wresting the knife out of his fingers.

"I'll take that, Zak," said a familiar voice close to his ear. "You might give yourself a nasty cut."

"Rina!" His voice came out in a gasp.

He twisted his head, startled at how close her fierce dark eyes were to his. "I've got it," he panted. "The memory stick. It's in my pocket."

She gave a wide grin. "Way to go, Zak!" she breathed. "Stay put."

Still holding the hunting knife, she padded down the stairs and kneeled at Blondie's side. She looked up at Zak. "Out for the count," she said. "You did good. Listen – see if you can find something to tie him up with. Rope or electric cable – or something." Her eyes shone in the gloom. "Quickly – we can't stay here. He won't be on his own."

Zak scrambled up the stairs. He rushed from room to room. There was a table lamp on the floor. Broken, but with a trailing cord. He ripped it away and ran back down to Rina.

She tied Blondie's wrists then turned him onto his side and pulled his feet up behind. She reeled out the remains of the cord and wrapped it around his ankles, tying it tightly.

"There," she said, standing. "That should slow him down." She looked up the stairwell. "Are you okay?"

Zak nodded, annoyed that he was still trembling slightly.

"Feel like giving me the memory stick?" she asked.

He pulled out the wallet and handed it to her. Rina flipped it open and took out the small stick, smiling and closing her fist around it. "Great!" she murmured, grinning at him. "Come on then, partner," she said. "Let's get out of here before this guy's pals show up."

CHAPTER **TWELVE**

The next few minutes were a kind of blur for Zak. It had been a long day and he was practically asleep on his feet. There was a flurry of activity as Rina bounded upstairs to retrieve her backpack, then a swift, silent exit through the back door of the house. A safari through an overgrown, weed-infested garden. A climb over a high brick wall. A stealthy trek across a series of well-kept lawns. A race down a side alley to a row of lock-up garages.

There were a few moments while Rina dealt with the padlocked door of one of the garages, then they dived under the semi-raised shutter door into pitch darkness.

Rina took a long slim length of something out of her backpack. She cracked it over her knee and it emitted a soft blue-white glow – giving them enough light to see what they were doing.

There was a car covered in a tarpaulin. There was a bench with tools. Bundles of stuff piled here and there. The smell of petrol.

Rina's large eyes looked even weirder in the eerie glow from the stick. She crouched, looking at Zak as he crumpled to the floor and leaned back against the wall.

He rallied himself, trying to keep his eyes open. "You can go to Hunter now," he said. "Give him the memory stick and prove it wasn't you."

"It's not quite that easy, Zak," she said. She leaned forwards, frowning – as if she was trying to make her mind up about something. "You did good," she said. "I'm sorry . . ." Her voice trailed away.

"Sorry about what?" he asked.

"Sorry you got involved."

He gave a weary smile. "Oh, that," he said. "It was fun. Kind of. In a totally terrifying way." His forehead contracted. "Except for Spizz . . . that wasn't any fun at all . . ." He rubbed his hands across his face, trying to wake up. "When we jumped into the river – did you think I'd drowned?"

She shook her head. "I saw you get picked up by the police boat," she said. "Did you tell them about me?"

"No, I didn't," said Zak. "But I did meet Hunter."

Her response was a sharp splinter of sound. "What?"

"He came to the police station – he took me to a place – an underground place. It was really strange down there."

"Fortress?" hissed Rina, leaning urgently forwards. "He took you to Fortress?"

"Is that what it's called?" Zak said.

"What happened?" Rina snapped. "What did you tell him? Why did he let you go?"

"He asked me a lot of questions – but I didn't tell him anything," Zak said. "Then I heard him planning to . . ." He paused, not liking to remember what he'd heard. "I climbed through a grille and legged it. Switchblade and a couple of others chased me. But they were way too slow." He grinned. "I came out near the Tower of London."

Rina frowned. "Yes, I know where you mean." Her eyes became slits as her eyebrows lowered. "He let you escape . . ." she murmured. "Why would he do that? So you'd lead him to me?"

Zak sat up. "You think I led Blondie to you?" he said in sudden dismay. "But how? I'd have seen him."

"Stand up!" Her voice was so harsh that Zak found himself on his feet almost before he had time to think about it. She kneeled in front of him, her hands moving roughly over him.

"What?" he asked.

"Did they put a bug on you?" she muttered.

"I don't think so . . ."

Her examination was thorough – she even made him take his shoes off so she could check them inside and underneath. She tried prizing the soles away too, but they were solid.

"Sit," she said, sounding relieved. "You're clean."

He sat down again. "I'm sorry," he said. "He must have followed me, but – honestly – I was careful. I never saw him."

Rina's voice was calm again. "No, you wouldn't," she said. "Don't sweat it, Zak. Everything's fine."

"So, what happens now?" Zak asked. "It's all okay, isn't it? You can take the stick to Colonel Hunter – and I can go home. Right?"

Rina grimaced. "I wish it was that easy – but I think we need to hang out together for a little while longer." She reached out and touched his knee with her long fingers. "Can I be completely honest with you, Zak?"

"Of course," he breathed.

"I don't think Hunter is one of the good guys," she said. "I think Switchblade copied the files on Hunter's orders. I think he's gone over to the other side."

Zak's eyes widened. Maybe she was right. Hunter had ordered him killed, after all. Good guys didn't do that.

"I need to get to Hunter's boss," Rina continued. "I have to convince him that the Controller of Project 17 is a traitor."

"Will he believe you?" asked Zak.

"I think so," Rina said. "But here's the thing, Zak – Hunter's boss isn't here right now. He's due in London early tomorrow morning. I have to lay low till he arrives – and I'd like you to stay with me till I meet up with him." She smiled again. "I wouldn't have got this far without you, Zak. You'd like to be in this at the end, wouldn't you?"

"I guess so . . ." he replied. "But that's not the reason you want me tagging along, is it?"

Her eyes glinted. 'What do you mean?"

"You think if I'm on my own I'll get picked up by Colonel Hunter again," Zak said. "You think I'll spill the beans about you."

Rina leaned in very close. "Not true," she said. She reached behind her and with a swift move, Blondie's knife was at his throat. "Trust me, Zak," she said. "If I thought that, I'd make sure you never spoke to anyone ever again. You know I'm capable of it, don't you?"

He nodded, swallowing hard.

She drew the knife away and tucked it into her backpack. "Did I scare you?" she asked.

"No . . . well . . . yes . . . sort of . . ." Zak stammered.

"I needed you to know I trust you," she said. "You'd already be dead if I didn't. We're sticking together because you can help me. Got it?"

He nodded again, his mouth suddenly dry. Rina had a scary way of making her point.

She took out her Mob and pressed the screen. "We should get some sleep," she said. "You look fried. We can catch a couple of hours before we have to go." She got up and went to the back of the garage. She returned a few moments later with some grubby dustsheets. "Not great," she admitted. "But it's the best I can do – and they'll keep us warm."

They made themselves as comfortable as they could, lying side by side on one of the folded sheets, draping the other over themselves.

"Tell me something, Zak," Rina said as they lay face to face. "Does this kind of life seem interesting to you?"

"Being a spy, you mean?" he murmured drowsily.

"Exactly."

He puzzled over this for a minute. Not sure what to say. Not sure what he thought.

Spizz's dead eyes asked him the same question.

His heavy eyes closed. He saw himself leaping from rooftop to rooftop – leaving Blondie and Pizza-face gasping for breath in his slipstream.

Now *that* had been fun . . .

"I guess so," he said at last.

The final thing he heard before he fell into a deep sleep was Rina's voice.

"Good," she said. "I think I might be able to help you there."

It felt as though he had only just closed his eyes when he was shaken awake.

"Rise and shine, partner." Rina's voice was too loud and too close to his ear. He blinked blearily, cold and stiff and sick of the whole thing. She pulled the dustsheet off him. "Places to go and people to see," she said, crouching and poking him with evil playfulness as he struggled to wake up. "Or do you want me to go without you?"

Yes – please do!

"No," he mumbled. "Give me a minute." He sat up,

rubbing his face with his hands. He needed a wash. Some fresh clothes. Breakfast. "What's the time?"

"Zero four hundred," Rina said. He stared blankly at her. "Four in the morning," she translated. "We have to get south of the river. Hunter's boss is due to arrive in an hour." She stood up, nudging him with her foot. "Shift yourself, Zak!"

She seemed in high spirits – a bit too high for four o'clock in the morning. But then she had good reason to be feeling cheerful – she was about to prove herself innocent. Zak just wished she could have done it a few hours later.

"Where are we meeting him?" Zak asked between yawns as he stood up and stretched.

"You'll see," said Rina. She stooped and pulled the shutter up. He followed her into the open. It was still dark and a thin mist hung in the air, grey and damp and chilly.

She looked him up and down. "Feeling fit?" she asked. Fit to drop.

"What's the plan?" he asked.

"An early morning jog," she said, bouncing on her toes. "You up for that, Zak?"

He nodded. He liked running in the early morning – all alone – just him and the wind and the open roads. But he liked it best after a good night's sleep in a warm bed.

Hitching her backpack high on her shoulders, Rina sprang away. Zak stared at her for a moment as she ran into the mist, then he caught his breath and went after her.

Zak and Rina jogged side by side through the streets. Zak had no idea where they were, but Rina seemed confident of the route. All he knew was that they were heading towards the Thames.

The minutes ticked by. An occasional car or van broke out of the mist, sending it swirling. They passed one or two other people out early, one of them walking a dog. It felt to Zak as if London was just waking – peering out from under the blankets – gathering itself for the coming day.

Gradually the mist thickened and became silvery as the sky lightened towards dawn. By the time they hit the River Thames, a dense fog shrouded them. It was clammy and dank and left droplets of moisture on their faces and arms as they crossed Battersea Bridge. Zak peered over the edge, his hair plastered to his forehead. The river was like a sheet of grey-brown hammered lead, thick and dense.

Rina checked her Mob. "Good," she panted. "Right on time." She glanced at him. "You just don't get tired, do you?"

Zak smiled but didn't reply. The impressed tone in her voice gave him a warm glow.

They came off the bridge and turned right, crossing a road and hitting a long fenced-in stretch of fog-shrouded trees. Zak had the feeling he knew this place. A park, maybe? London was a big city. Zak only knew parts of it well.

Rina didn't hesitate for a moment. She ran for the railings, bounced high and boosted herself over with both hands. She looked back at him through the iron rails.

"Come on – we're almost there," she said.

He sprang up, following her over the railings.

"Where are we?" Zak asked.

"The Millennium Arena," Rina replied. "Know it?"

"Yes." Of course he did – he'd just never approached it from this direction before. And the fog didn't help.

It was a sports club with facilities for track and field events as well as football pitches and tennis courts. There was also an indoor fitness centre with a well-equipped gym and various rooms for judo and karate and stuff like that. He'd been there a couple of times with other people from the home. It had an eight-lane running track – it was a good place to burn off some energy. But it seemed a weird spot for Rina to be meeting with Colonel Hunter's boss.

They came to the edge of the trees. The fog rolled slowly over a wide flat area of grass. Zak could just about make out the tennis courts with their high wire fences. Beyond them, the red rubber running track curved away into grey nothingness.

Rina paused, swinging the backpack off her shoulders and taking out something that looked like a large digital camera. She held it to her eye and made a long, slow sweep of the open area in front of them.

"Heat-seeking camera," she explained. "Just checking we don't have any unwanted visitors." She smiled. "Take a look."

He held the camera to his eye. All he could see was a blue blur.

"People show up red and yellow," Rina explained, taking the camera back. She looked at him. "Remember what I asked you last night?" she said. "About this spy game?"

He nodded.

"Play your cards right, and I might be able to put in a good word for you," she said. "Would you like that?"

The question made his head spin. After all he'd been through, the last thing he wanted was to get caught up in even more of this dangerous spy stuff. He just wanted to go home.

Rina's head snapped around. "Hold up!" she hissed. "I think we have incoming."

Zak frowned, listening.

He heard the faint *whumph-whumph* of helicopter blades. A cold fear trickled through him.

"It's fine," Rina said, taking his hand. "Come on. It's the good guys."

She led him from under the trees. The noise of the approaching helicopter grew louder. He looked up into the grey sky.

There it was! A dark blur through the fog, flying low, creating spiralling tornados of white air as it came in for a landing.

Rina was running now, towing Zak behind her. Excited. Her fingers digging into his palm.

The helicopter landed on the oval field of grass within the curve of the running track. The steady, deafening beat of the rotor blades slowed.

Keeping low, Rina and Zak moved closer. Zak winced – she was holding his hand very tightly.

A door opened in the side of the helicopter and a short

set of metal steps thudded down into the grass. A man appeared in the doorway. Tall, olive-skinned, with dark buzz-cut hair and a golden earring. Even in the dim light, Zak could tell he was wearing an expensive suit suit. He stepped down and walked towards them, ignoring the sweeping rotor blades. He gave Zak a quick, curious glance then looked at Rina and smiled.

"Good morning, Ballerina," he said. He had a slight accent, but Zak couldn't pin it down. Middle Eastern, maybe?

"Hello, Barracuda," Rina said.

"I am sorry to have kept you waiting, my dear friend," Barracuda continued. "As I'm sure my representative told you, urgent business detained me in Kiev for longer than I had anticipated." The man's eyeline changed, as though he had spotted something behind them. "Ahhh," he said. "What have we here?"

Zak turned his head. A figure was moving out of the fog.

His heart pounded. "Rina! Watch out!" he yelled.

It was Blondie. And he was holding a gun.

"Chill out, Zak," said Rina, her fingernails knifing into his hand. "We're all friends here."

Zak stared at Rina in alarm. Something was wrong — horribly wrong. Had she set him up? He'd trusted her right from the beginning. He'd defended her to Hunter. He couldn't believe this was happening.

He struggled to get away from her, but she flicked a foot out and at the same moment, hit his shoulder with the flat of her hand, tipping him over so he went crashing onto the grass.

As he lay gasping, he saw the three of them looking down at him. Blondie's gun was aimed at his forehead.

Rina grinned at him. "Well now, Zak," she said. "Ever get the feeling you've been had?"

CHAPTER **THIRTEEN**

Zak looked at the three faces in a kind of daze. He couldn't believe what had happened. It didn't make any sense.

The helicopter rotor blades scythed the air, making the fog swirl, giving the whole scene an unreal look. As if he'd fallen into a bad, bad dream.

"I'll shoot him now," said Blondie. "We can dump the body over the sea on the way out."

"No, don't do that," said Rina. "He might be useful."

"You should introduce our guest," said Barracuda. "Pick him up, Ballerina. Where are your manners?"

Rina reached down and hauled Zak to his feet. He glared at her, pulling away. She smiled and shrugged, holding her hands up and stepping back.

"His name is Zak Archer," she told Barracuda. "He's a little street rat who's been helping me out." She winked at Zak. "He can't fight his way out of a paper bag – but he can run like nothing you've ever seen."

Barracuda looked at him appraisingly. "Will he be useful to us, do you think?" he asked.

"I think he might," said Rina. "Given the right incentives."

"I'm standing right here!" Zak spat. He felt angry and hurt and betrayed and helpless all at the same time. "And I'm never going to help you." He gave Rina a look of pure loathing. "You lied to me right from the start."

"Oh, come on, Zak, don't be a poor loser," she said. "Play your cards right and we can all come out of this smelling of roses." She turned to Barracuda. "He's smart and very tenacious, and he learns quick," she said. "But he's kind of gullible, and he has a bad case of the goody two-shoes."

Barracuda smiled. "We have ways of knocking those particular faults out of people," he said. He nodded. "Very well – we take him with us." His voice became sharp and hard. "Do you have the goods, Ballerina?"

A grin stretched across Rina's face and she jerked her thumb towards the backpack that hung from her shoulders. The wallet with the memory stick in it was in one of the side pockets. "Would I let you down?" she said.

Barracuda's eyes became icy. "You had best not, my dear," he said. He turned to Blondie. "Let us be on our way – I have no wish to give Hunter and his pack the opportunity to—"

The sudden roar of a car engine cut off his words. He twisted, staring into the fog with a ferocious look on his face. Zak heard the sound of skidding wheels. Black shapes hurtled out of the fog – two, three, four big dark transit vans, their headlights raking through the fog, their engines revving.

"You fool!" Barracuda spat at Rina. She was standing with her eyes wide in disbelief. With a snarl, Barracuda ran for the helicopter, shouting something in a foreign language. The doors of the black vans sprang open and dark shapes came pouring out. Blondie backed towards the helicopter, his gun arm swinging as though he couldn't decide on a target.

Rina seemed to come back to herself. She burst into motion, running hard for the gap between two of the vans.

Zak threw himself down behind Blondie, snatching at his ankles. The big man tottered for a moment then crashed to the ground. A moment later a black-clad figure was on top of him. The gun was wrested from his hand. An arm rose and fell. Blondie grunted and stopped moving.

Zak scrambled to his feet, his hair whipping about his face as the rotor blades of the helicopter sped up. The door was closed – Barracuda was inside. The helicopter's engine rose to a deafening crescendo as the aircraft lifted off.

Someone was shouting. Shots rang out, whining as they struck off the helicopter's hull.

Zak turned to where he had last seen Rina, running between two of the vans – but she had been swallowed in the fog. He had to stop her. She'd betrayed him – he wasn't going to let her get away with it.

He raced away, darting past the figures, diving between the vans. He could hear the sound of the helicopter rising further into the sky. There were more shots.

The powerful rhythm of the helicopter's engine stuttered and the note changed to a high-pitched whine. The beat of the blades faltered. His heart in his mouth, Zak glanced over his shoulder.

The helicopter was hanging in the sky at a strange angle, the engine screaming, the rotor blades slowing, flames flickering from the fuselage. It tipped sideways and plunged at a raking slant towards Zak.

With a yell of panic, he kicked off, racing across the grass, every ounce of strength and muscle working to get him away from the falling machine.

He would never make it. The helicopter would crush him.

Then he heard the terrible sound of the stricken aircraft hitting the ground at his back. The earth shook as the burning hot blast wave lifted Zak off his feet and sent him tumbling through the air.

He curled himself into a ball as the shock of the explosion bowled him over and over across the grass until he came to a sprawling halt.

When he finally staggered up, the helicopter was a ball of flame. A plume of black smoke was rising into the sky. No one could have survived a crash like that.

Zak stumbled backwards – shaken and numb – one hand up to protect his face from the searing heat.

Then he remembered Rina.

He spun on his heel. There was no sign of her.

Undaunted, he ran into the fog, picking up speed, letting the gears mesh. He'd catch her. No one could outrun him.

The fitness centre loomed up ahead, a big grey brick building near the road. He moved faster, his arms pumping, his legs propelling him along like well-oiled pistons.

Rina wasn't going to get away. Not after what she'd put him through today.

He came bombing around the corner of the building, moving at top speed, fuelled by anger and revenge.

A band of solid darkness snapped out in front of him. It struck him on the chest, winding him, sending him spinning, gasping for breath with a sucking vacuum where his lungs should be.

He slammed to the ground and skidded across biting gravel. Pain roared through his body. Red flares detonated behind his eyes, blinding him. He lay face down, panting and moaning in pain. It felt as though all the skin had been taken off his hands and knees.

Suddenly he was grabbed from behind and tipped onto his back. Rina towered over him, her expression furious, her eyes burning.

She thudded down on top of him, pinning him.

"You should have let me get away," she hissed, her face close to his. "I really didn't want to have to kill you, Zak."

One hand came to his throat. She squeezed. Black holes opened up in front of his eyes. The pain was overwhelming.

But from somewhere deep within, Zak found the strength to twist his aching body to one side. Rina overbalanced, her hand loosening at his throat. He dragged himself away from her, coughing and choking.

She scrambled up, reaching for the backpack on her shoulders. Now there was a knife in her fist. Blondie's big hunting knife.

Zak pushed himself away as she moved in.

A voice called through the fog. "I saw him go this way!"

An answering shout. "Where?"

"Over here!"

Rina's head snapped around and her eyes narrowed. People were coming.

Rina's eyes drilled into him. "This isn't over," she said. The next moment she disappeared into the mist.

Zak pulled himself into a sitting position with his back to the grey wall. He felt as if he'd been through a blender. There was blood on his hands. The knees of his jeans were ripped. He hurt all over.

Switchblade raced around the corner. He came to a stuttering halt as he caught sight of Zak.

Zak pointed. "That way."

With a quick nod, Switchblade ran off into the mist.

Zak noticed something lying in the disturbed gravel. A wallet. He crawled over and picked it up. Rina's wallet! It must have fallen out of the pocket of her backpack as they had tussled. He opened it. The memory stick was still inside.

He couldn't quite believe it.

A second figure appeared. Colonel Hunter, dressed all in black, his grey hair covered with a black beret. He kneeled at Zak's side.

"Are you hurt?" he asked.

Zak grimaced.

"Can you stand?"

Zak tried to get up. Colonel Hunter put a hand under his arm to help. Zak leaned against the wall, dizzy and still a little stunned from his fall.

"She tricked me," he murmured. "But she dropped this." He handed the wallet to Colonel Hunter. "The memory stick is inside."

The Colonel looked carefully into his face. "Good work," he said. "Come with me. Let's get you fixed up."

With shaking legs and a light head, Zak allowed himself to be led back to the vans. The helicopter was still burning fiercely, but the battle was over. Blondie was in handcuffs, being loaded into one of the vehicles. The black figures were standing in small groups, waiting for orders.

Zak sat in the doorway of one of the vans, feeling sick and hurt and tired. All the excitement was gone now, he just felt stupid that he'd let Rina use him.

Colonel Hunter stood at his side, speaking into a Mob.

Switchblade jogged towards them.

"No luck," he panted. "She managed to flag down a motorbike – threw the rider off – and then she was away." His face contracted in anger. "I didn't even get close."

"We'll pick her up later," said Hunter. "She can't do too much harm now – Zak got the memory stick."

Switchblade looked impressed. "Way to go, Zak!"

Zak smiled wearily, too whacked to feel pleased with himself. And too worn down by the day's events to be sure he was even trusting the right people now. Not that it seemed they were giving him any other choice.

Colonel Hunter pocketed his Mob. "Okay, people," he called. "We're done here. Team Alpha: wait for the fire brigade. Clean up. Keep the public away. The rest of you – move out."

Zak was bundled into the back of the van with a few others. The door slammed. The motor revved and the van went bouncing away across the grass.

Zak curled himself up on the floor of the van. He had no idea where he was being taken. He was too exhausted even to care.

CHAPTER **FOURTEEN**

Zak woke up in a strange bed in a strange room. For a moment he had no idea where he was or how he had got here. The room was small and clean in a clinical kind of way – a hospital, perhaps? Was he ill? He didn't feel ill.

Halogen lights glowed in the ceiling. There were no windows in the plain white walls. The door was closed.

Wincing, he pushed the bed covers away. He ached all over and there were some nasty grazes on the palms of his hands.

Then it all came flooding back. The uncomfortable

journey in the black van. Being half-carried through a doorway. Going down in a lift, surrounded by people in black. Then there were doctors and nurses and worried, friendly faces.

He remembered saying over and over. "I trusted her – I'm sorry – tell Colonel Hunter I'm sorry."

They did tests on him and took blood samples and put him in some kind of large machine and told him to keep very still while they scanned his body from top to toe. Then he was put to bed in this room. Then he lost track.

He sat up. A camera lens winked from a corner of the ceiling. He stared blankly into it.

You idiot! You are in so much trouble now. They'll think you were working with her. They're going to lock you up and throw away the key – and no one will ever know what happened to you.

He saw some clothes piled neatly on a chair. Not his own clothes, but they looked as if they'd fit.

There was a knock on the door.

He stared at it. Waiting. Silent. Apprehensive.

Another knock.

He swallowed hard. "Come in."

The door opened. A woman in a white coat entered, carrying a tray.

"How are you feeling this morning, Zak?" she asked briskly, laying the tray on his legs. There was orange juice. Scrambled eggs on toast. A bowl of cereal and a jug of milk.

"Okay," he said guardedly.

"Good." She nodded at the tray. "Eat up," she said.

"What day is it?" he asked.

"It's Tuesday morning. Seven-thirty."

The showdown at the Millennium Arena had been early on Monday. He'd slept through an entire day!

"People at the home will be worried about me," he told her.

"No, they won't," said the woman. "They know you're safe. Eat your breakfast. You have half an hour till your Appraisal Meeting."

He stared up at her. "Till my what?"

"Eat up," she repeated. "I'll be back in a while."

She walked to the door and closed it behind her. Zak gazed at the closed door for a few moments, then looked into the camera on the wall.

The scrambled eggs smelled good.

Appraisal Meeting? What was that? Like a trial?

Zachary Archer has been found guilty of the most horrible crime of treachery against his country. In light of his heinous actions, I have no option but to . . .

No. Let's not go there.

He looked down at the tray.

Hungry, despite everything. He must have missed a few meals while he'd been out of it.

He began to eat. What else was there to do?

It wasn't the woman in the white coat who came back. It was Switchblade.

Zak had finished his breakfast and got dressed. He was sitting on the edge of the bed, tying his shoelaces when the door opened.

"Good – you're up," Switchblade said. "Come on – everyone is waiting."

"Waiting for what?" Zak asked, eyeing the tall blue-eyed boy uneasily.

"For you," said Switchblade. He didn't smile, but he didn't look angry either. "Move yourself, Control doesn't like to be kept hanging around."

"Control?" Zak asked in bemusement.

"Colonel Hunter."

"Oh. Him." Zak didn't feel up to arguing. He followed Switchblade into a white corridor.

"I'm sorry I whacked you over the head," he said as they walked along.

Switchblade glanced at him. "Don't sweat it," he said. "It was nothing."

Zak frowned. "I knocked you out," he reminded him.

Switchblade grinned now. "With that bit of rotten old wood?" he said. "You must be kidding. I faked it so you'd get away. You didn't even leave a scratch."

Zak was baffled. "Why did you do that?"

"Control's orders," Switchblade explained. "Ballerina is smart. She'd have smelled a rat if she thought we weren't hunting for her. So I was sent to pick a fight – and to lose. You just made it easier for me to go down."

"Oh, I see," said Zak. But he didn't. Not really.

"Confused?" asked Switchblade.

"Totally," Zak admitted.

"Take everything Ballerina told you and flip it," Switchblade recommended. "Believe the exact opposite. That'll be a good start. Colonel Hunter will fill in the rest." He stopped outside a plain door with P.17.L.02. printed on it. "This is it," he said, pushing the door open. "Welcome to Project 17."

Zak was sitting in a swivel chair in the middle of a very modern, high-tech room. He had the curious sensation of his brain whirling around and around inside his head as he tried to take in what he was being told.

Switchblade and a small, quiet boy with a deep fringe were sitting behind him, along with a couple of adults wearing white coats. There was a huge plasma screen on the wall in front of him. Colonel Hunter was standing to one side, clicking a handheld device to show Zak a series of moving images – mostly of him and Rina running through dark streets and across rooftops, sometimes seen through the lens of CCTV cameras, and sometimes as aerial shots – presumably from a helicopter.

"We've been aware of Ballerina's plans for several months," said Colonel Hunter. "Ever since Bug here intercepted a transmission she made to a gentleman known to us by the codename Barracuda."

Zak glanced over his shoulder but the small boy called Bug was busy working on something that looked like an iPad, and he didn't even look up.

"Barracuda was the guy in the helicopter at the Millennium Arena," Zak offered, doing his best to seem less lost in all this than he felt.

"Yes, he was," said the Colonel. "He runs the espionage unit of a very dangerous foreign power – we've been after him for a long time."

"I think you got him," Zak mumbled.

"I think we did," agreed the Colonel.

"Good and crispy," added Switchblade. "Barbecued Barracuda on a sesame seed bun. Very tasty!"

The Colonel frowned at him. "Alive would have been better, but at least he's been neutralized." He clicked the remote and more scenes appeared of Zak and Rina on the run.

"Ballerina was a smart agent," Colonel Hunter continued. "But she overestimated herself and underestimated us. She thought her Mob was fitted with a jamming device – but Bug tinkered with it so it let out a homing signal instead."

"So you were following her all the time?" said Zak, ruefully remembering his mobile phone being flushed.

"We had her on a long leash, Zak," said the Colonel. "We wanted her to lead us to Barracuda. As far as she knew, things started to unravel when Barracuda was held up abroad. She'd expected to meet with him late last week – and by the time she found out he'd be two days late, she had no time to change her plans.

"That gave us the time we needed to set up the sting," continued Colonel Hunter. "Ballerina went to ground in Ladbroke Grove, and waited in an abandoned house for Barracuda's men to contact her with instructions about when and where he'd meet her."

"And we were listening in on the whole thing," said Switchblade. "Thanks to Bug's mega-computer-geekiness."

Bug was busy with his electronic device and he didn't react to Switchblade's joke.

"She arranged to meet two of Barracuda's men on Sunday at noon in a games arcade," said Colonel Hunter. "From there, she'd be taken to the pick-up point."

Zak's eyes widened as he finally understood about Blondie and Pizza-face. "They weren't sent by you at all," he said. "They were there to get the memory stick from Rina. And Spizz totally wrecked their plans when he swiped Rina's wallet with the memory stick in it."

"He did," said the Colonel. "And he paid for it with his life." His face became grim. "We were very sorry about that, Zak – believe me. We never intended any civilians to come to harm."

"He always took risks," said Zak. "I liked him, but he was always looking for trouble. I just wish he hadn't found it. Not like that, anyway." He looked thoughtfully at the Colonel. "When you left me in that room – I heard you talking on the phone. You faked that, didn't you – you were never going to have me killed."

"I was testing your initiative," said the Colonel. "I wanted to see if you'd try to escape."

"And you did," added Switchblade. "It was very impressive."

"And when Rina first grabbed me," said Zak, looking at the Colonel. "You were one of the people in the black van at Robert Wyatt House, weren't you?"

Colonel Hunter nodded. "We wanted to protect you," he said. "I'd hoped we could get to you before she did – but we missed it by a few minutes."

"And all her talk about Sweeper Teams?" asked Zak. "That wasn't true either."

"Nope," said Switchblade. "She wanted to keep you off balance. So you wouldn't trust anyone but her."

"Someone shot at us – when we were under the bridge," said Zak. "Who was that?"

"Not us," said the Colonel. "I think Barracuda's men were losing patience. The shot was a reminder to her that she needed to get the memory stick back pronto."

Zak remembered how she'd used her Mob shortly after he'd told her about Dodge. She must have been letting her pals know where to meet up and get the stick. Then Dodge hadn't been there under the arches – but she didn't have time to call Barracuda's men off before they arrived.

She couldn't risk Zak finding out the truth until she had the stick back – so she'd run, pretending her nasty pals were one of Colonel Hunter's non-existent Sweeper Teams.

That also explained why Blondie had been in the boarded-up house in Ladbroke Grove. He hadn't followed Zak! He'd been there to meet Rina.

"She could have killed me once I'd given her the stick," Zak said, vividly remembering the incident with the knife in the garage. "But she didn't – she kept me with her."

The Colonel nodded. "I think that by then she'd seen the potential in you, Zak," he said. "Just like we have." He beckoned and one of the two white coats got up and came to the front. He looked nervous and blinked a lot from behind thick horn-rimmed glasses. "Except that we now have a much clearer idea of how you've come to be so fast," continued the Colonel. "Thanks to Doctor Jackson's tests."

"I don't know that I'm all *that* fast," Zak muttered.

"Yes, you do," said Colonel Hunter. "No false modesty, Zak. It has no purpose here."

"When you're in the zone, you're crazy fast, and you know it," added Switchblade.

In the zone. Yes – that was a good way of putting it.

"Doctor Jackson will explain," said the Colonel, handing over the remote.

The doctor clicked the remote and CCTV footage appeared on screen of Zak and Rina racing across rooftops, Rina always in the rear – especially when it came to the long jumps from roof to roof.

"We've analysed these pictures, and we've found that for short bursts you can run at over forty kilometres an hour," said the doctor, blinking at Zak through his horn-rimmed glasses. "That is incredibly fast. In fact it's unheard of in a boy of your age." The picture changed to a circle with pinkish blobby-looking liquid swishing around. "From our tests, we've learned that you suffer from a chemical imbalance in your adrenal glands." There was a change of picture to a weird set of prints of slices of his body and head in freaky colours. "These brain scans from the MRI machine show the effect of the adrenaline burst. Our initial analysis suggests that your body secretes almost double the usual amount of adrenaline when you are in stressful or hyper-alert situations."

Zak started at the screen. "Is that bad?" he asked anxiously.

The doctor took off his glasses and polished them frantically with a handkerchief. "Normally, it would be very dangerous indeed," he said. "That kind of thing would very quickly shred a normal human system – but somehow your body compensates and manages to use the extra adrenaline to its advantage. It's unique. I've never seen anything quite like it before." He glanced at the Colonel. "Under other circumstances, I'd want to make a more thorough investigation and publish the results." He looked a bit gloomy. "But Control tells me that isn't going to be possible."

Zak was alarmed now. "Is it going to kill me?" he gulped.

"Quite the reverse," said the doctor, pushing his glasses back on. "You are remarkable healthy – in fact, with the proper guidance and training, I think it's entirely possible that you will be able to take full control of your body's unusual abilities." He blinked at Zak. "I think you've only scratched the surface of what you're capable of, young man."

Zak sat back in surprise. "Oh," he said. "That's good . . . I mean . . . it is, isn't it?"

Colonel Hunter smiled. "It could be very good," he said. "But that's going to be up to you, Zak."

Zak looked at him, not sure what he was getting at.

"There's a gap in our ranks now Ballerina's gone," said Switchblade. "Control is inviting you to try out for Project 17." He leaned forwards, nudging Zak's arm with his fist. "What do you say, Zak? Want to join up?"

Not for the first time in the past couple of days, Zak didn't know what to say.

"There's no pressure," Switchblade said as he walked Zak along another of those white corridors. "It's up to you – either you join Project 17, or you go back to your old life as if nothing had happened."

"And I have *how* long to make my mind up?" Zak asked. He'd lost track of what the Colonel had said to him following that Big Question that Zak hadn't been able to answer.

"Twenty-four hours," Switchblade told him. He glanced mischievously at Zak. "Of course, you realize that if you turn us down, Control will take you to the Mind Warp room where all your memories of this place will be surgically removed from your brain." He shrugged. "Don't sweat it, though – most people come out of it fine – more or less. There's some drooling. Loss of balance. That kind of thing."

Zak gave him a horrified look and Switchblade burst out laughing.

"Just kidding," he said. "There's no surgery. They do it with lasers – they zap 'em straight into your brain through your skull. The memories are burned out and—"

"Oh, shut up!" said Zak. "There's no Mind Warp room."

Switchblade grinned. "Wouldn't it be great if there was, though?" he said. "No, the truth is, if you don't want a life filled with thrills and spills and high-octane excitement, that's just fine. You can walk away. And you can talk about this place and about Project 17 to whoever you like – no one is going to believe you."

"I could post on the Internet," Zak suggested. "People believe anything they see on the Internet."

"You could try," said Switchblade. "But Bug would track your post down in five minutes flat and shut you down in six." Switchblade looked at him keenly, and there was no trace of humour in his voice now. "And afterwards – probably within an hour – some officials will turn up at your home and you'll be whisked off to a special place for disturbed and delusional kids. And you'll have a beard down to your waist before you see daylight again."

"Not kidding this time?" asked Zak.

"Not kidding," Switchblade confirmed.

"But if I just go away and say nothing, I'll be left alone, right?"

Switchblade nodded. "It's happened before," he said. "And even if you do take Control up on his offer, you'd only have a one in ten chance of making it through the training schedule. Most people burn out halfway through the physical – then there's the academic stuff." He shook his head. "If I were you, I'd tell Control no way. Get out now, Zak, while the getting's good."

Zak gave him a long look. "You passed the tests, right?" he said.

"I did."

Zak shrugged. "So, how hard can it be?"

Switchblade laughed. "Good answer," he said.

"Colonel Hunter said you'd tell me all about this place," said Zak. "So – what's the story?"

"From what you've said, Rina pretty much told you the truth about us," Switchblade said as he led Zak into a room with a large modern map of London on the wall. "We're a small specialist team of young people who take on missions where an adult would stand out too much." He gestured at the map. It was very detailed, showing all the main streets and side streets, with the blue snake of the River Thames winding between. Railways stations and tube stops and places of special interest like the Houses of Parliament and Buckingham Palace were marked with flags and stickers.

"The underground complex we're in was originally used by Churchill's government . . ." Switchblade began.

"During the Second World War," Zak interrupted. "I know that."

"History geek?" asked Switchblade.

"I watch the History Channel sometimes," Zak explained.

Switchblade's eyebrows rose. "Most kids your age would be watching music videos and cartoons."

Kids your age? Like Switch was more than a year or two older than him!

"I do that, too," Zak said. He walked up to the huge map. "What are these?" he asked, pointing at four large round blue circles that didn't seem to represent anything so far as he could tell.

Switchblade rapped his knuckles against one of the circles. "That's us," he said. "Fortress. The main areas are under Moorgate, but we have links to the other three zones." He hit the map again at the blue circle that surrounded Waterloo station. "That's Rampart." He pointed to the third and fourth rings. "The complex under St Paul's Cathedral is called Citadel – and the one beneath Covent Garden is Bastion."

So – there was another of these secret underground cities right under where Dodge lived in his hardboard home. That was a weird thought. Dodge and his down-and-out pals living their meagre lives under the railway arches, while beneath their feet a whole army of spies was racing around saving the world.

"And all this is Project 17?" Zak breathed, astonished at the scope of the excavations.

"No – we're located in Fortress," Switchblade replied.

"And who's in the others?" asked Zak.

Switchblade lifted an eyebrow. "That's something you don't need to know," he said. "All I'm authorized to tell you about is Project 17 – and even then, there's plenty of cool stuff I can't show you." He smiled. "Of course, if you agree to take the training courses, and *if* you pass, then you'll find out a whole bunch more – and you'll get to meet the rest of the guys."

Zak looked at him. "I met two of them, I think – a girl with blond hair and black lipstick, and a big guy with muscles."

Switchblade nodded. "Wildcat and Jackhammer," he said. "They're off-base now – helping to hunt down Ballerina. And there's Moonbeam – she's on a mission in Kuala Lumpur. Tripwire and Icewater are in Berlin. The others are all over."

Kuala Lumpur? Berlin? Zak's head was beginning to spin again. How could he turn this opportunity down? Anyone else would jump at the chance.

But would they if they'd seen a friend get chucked

off a gantry? Would they if they kept seeing Spizz's dead eyes in their head? Warning them of what could happen. Warning them that this wasn't a game.

Before he made his mind up he wanted the chance to speak with the one person whose advice he valued above all others. He wanted to speak to Dodge.

"So?" asked Switchblade. "Seen enough? Want to go away and think it over now?"

Zak nodded.

"You know what to do when you want to contact us?" asked Switchblade.

"Yes." The Colonel had given him a small grey device, about the size of a credit card. It had a touch-sensitive number pad on it. When he'd made his mind up he had been told to key in the numbers 3005 and then stay put.

Switchblade took him up in a lift and along another of those bare concrete corridors without any rooms off it.

He thought he recognized the way, but he couldn't be sure. "Last time I was here," he said, looking sidelong at Switchblade. "You guys let me escape, didn't you?"

"You'd never have got out by yourself, I'll tell you that much," said Switchblade.

"Maybe not, but I'd have given you a run for your

money," Zak replied.

"Yes, you would," agreed Switchblade. "You're a nippy one, Zak."

They came to a steel door. Switchblade opened a metal box set on the wall. He pressed his hand to a blue screen within the box. There was a soft click and the door swung open to reveal a filthy brick-built tunnel streaked with daylight that filtered down through gratings.

"Nervous?" asked Switchblade.

"No." Zak looked at him. "Should I be?"

"Ballerina is still out there," Switchblade said. "She's vindictive, Zak. She'll blame you for messing up her plans. I'd watch my back if I were you."

Zak frowned at him. "I hadn't thought of that," he said. "Thanks a bunch for putting that idea in my head."

"No sweat," said Switchblade. "She's probably out of the country already. You'll be fine."

Or not?

"There's a hatch about fifty metres along," Switchblade said, pointing down the tunnel. "There shouldn't be any people where you come out. But remember to close the hatch after you." Zak stepped through the door and Switchblade swung it closed. "Maybe I'll see you later, Quicksilver," he said through the narrowing gap.

Zak turned his head sharply. "What did you call me?"

Switchblade's eyes flashed with humour. "If you join Project 17, Control thinks you should have the codename Quicksilver," he said.

And then the door closed with a clang and Zak was alone.

CHAPTER **FIFTEEN**

Zak didn't go straight back to Robert Wyatt House. He wasn't sure exactly why. Maybe it was because he didn't want to have to meet up with Spizz's close friends and try to explain to them what had happened. Maybe it was because he didn't feel like being taken aside by Kath or Paul and quizzed about where he'd been since Sunday morning. Sure, Colonel Hunter said they'd been told he was in protective custody following Spizz's death – but they'd want the details. He wasn't at all sure he was ready for that.

Or maybe he didn't go back because he didn't like

the idea of the people at Project 17 watching him every step of the way on CCTV.

Besides, he knew a place where there weren't any cameras. A place where he could be on his own to run and think and make the biggest decision of his entire life.

Zak sped through the trees on Hampstead Heath, leaping the bracken, vaulting fallen trunks, negotiating the rise and fall of the landscape at top speed.

In the zone.

He liked that phrase.

When the gears meshed he was definitely *in the zone*.

The sky was burning blue above the canopy of leaves. There was no sound of traffic. No CCTV surveillance. No helicopters. Nothing but him and the way ahead and the blood pumping in his veins and the wind singing in his ears.

Perfect!

And yet . . .

It was stupid, he knew – but he couldn't shake the nasty feeling that he was being followed. Shadowed. Tracked.

Paranoia.

He glanced over his shoulder, peering through the trees. There was no one there.

All the same, he'd been aware of an unpleasant burning between his shoulder blades ever since he'd left the tunnel. That same feeling of being in the cross hairs that had been with him all day. A target. It had followed him to the tube station and all the way on the underground train to Hampstead station.

"This is all Switchblade's fault!" he muttered to himself as he ran on. Putting ideas in his head. Freaking him out.

Something swung suddenly across his path – like a long black arm coming from behind a tree. He just had time to throw his hands up to save himself from being struck in the face.

The impact of the thing sent him spinning to the ground, winded and half-stunned. A thick branch rose above him. It came sweeping down. He rolled to one side as the branch cracked hard on the ground where his head had been.

Zak sprang to his feet, leaping back as Rina swung the branch again, the club-like end only missing his chest by a fraction.

She looked bad. She'd obviously been sleeping rough. Her hair was matted and tangled around her face, and her eyes were red-rimmed and burning with vengeance.

And Zak had put himself in the one place where there

was no one to watch over him – the one place where Rina could take her revenge without being seen. His dead body left to be sniffed out by someone's dog – tomorrow, or the day after, or the day after that.

Zak turned and sprinted, the blood pounding in his head as he leaped through the trees. But his fear betrayed him; he caught his foot on a hidden root and went stumbling sideways into a tree.

Something sliced the skin of his upper arm, making him cry out, pinning him to the tree. It was Blondie's hunting knife. Rina had thrown it, just grazing him, impaling his sleeve to the trunk. He tried desperately to drag himself free.

He heard crashing through the bracken. Rina was coming for him.

With a final effort, he ripped himself loose and staggered away, clutching his arm, feeling the blood warm between his fingers.

"No!" Rina hardly sounded human. "No!"

He flicked a glance back. Rina had pulled the knife from the tree as she ran past – she was coming after him. He stumbled on, but the pain in his arm made it hard to concentrate – hard to get into the zone.

He crashed into a rearing hedge. Spiked branches tore at him. With a cry, Rina was on him. Her weight bore down on his back, sending him hurtling forwards.

As he fell through the cracking branches, he was aware of emptiness under his hands. The ground plunged down a long steep drop into a deep, bracken-choked ditch.

The two of them tumbled over and over down the steep slope, Rina clinging to him as they fell.

He hit bottom first, and Rina came down heavily on top of him. She gave a low guttural gasp, her body limp and awkward across his. He lay panting under her, the blood hammering in his head.

She didn't move. Gathering his wits, Zak slid out from under her and got to his knees. She rolled onto her back in the undergrowth. Blondie's hunting knife was sticking out of her side just under her ribs.

With a cry of horror, Zak scrambled away from her. Hardly knowing what he was doing, he clawed his way up the steep slope, hands and feet digging in as he clambered out of the ditch and forced his way back through the hedge.

He came out into the open and almost cannoned into Switchblade.

"She's down there . . ." he gasped, doubled over, fighting for breath, too scared to be surprised that Switch was there. "I think she's dead."

Switchblade nodded and plunged into the wreckage of the hedge. Zak fell to his knees, shaking, feeling sick. Threads of blood ran down his arm from the shallow knife wound. He could hear Switchblade going down the hill.

There was silence. Zak gritted his teeth, and made himself stand up again. He shoved his way through the hedge to the lip of the fall. Switchblade was down there – but there was no sign of Rina.

Zak watched as Switchblade clambered up the long slope. "There's blood on the ground," he said. "But she wasn't dead." His eyes narrowed as he saw the blood on Zak's arm. "She got you?" he asked.

"Just a small cut," said Zak. "Were you following me all the way?"

"Yes, sorry," Switchblade said. "I've been right behind you ever since you left Fortress. We didn't want to risk something like this happening."

"You could have told me," breathed Zak.

"You might have tried to slip me," Switchblade explained. "You're an independent kind of person, Zak. We know that." He put his hand on Zak's shoulder. "Come on – there's a van waiting. Let's get you patched up."

"She was going to kill me," Zak mumbled as he walked along at Switchblade's side, one hand holding his injured arm. "I think she's gone mental."

"She won't be in a fit state to try anything for a while," said Switchblade. "Besides, we've got your back now, Quicksilver."

Zak looked at him. "Don't call me that," he said.

Switchblade gave him a surprised and disappointed look. "You're not with us?"

"I don't know," said Zak. "I haven't made my mind up yet."

"What should I do, Dodge?" Zak asked.

The two friends were sitting on a bench on the embankment of the River Thames, eating hotdogs and watching the boats coming and going under the hot midday sun. Zak's arm had been patched up and it hardly even hurt now.

"What do you *want* to do, Zachary?" Dodge replied, wiping his hands on a napkin then balling it up and lobbing it expertly into a nearby bin. "That's the real question."

Zak sighed. "I wish I knew."

"If wishes were horses, beggars would ride," Dodge said, spreading his arms along the back of the bench and turning his face to the sunlight.

Zak had found his friend in his old haunt under the

arches of Waterloo station. He'd wanted Dodge to know the whole story, and after swearing him to secrecy, he'd explained everything in detail as they walked together.

Dodge had paid careful attention, bringing Zak up sharp when he'd missed out something important, and asking some searching questions, especially when it came to Project 17 and Colonel Hunter.

Zak finished his hotdog, scrunched the napkin up and threw it. It bounced off the rim of the bin. He walked over, picked it up and dropped it in the bin.

"I can't decide," he said. "I mean – it's not like my life is so very great the way it is . . . but at least I'm not getting shot at and stabbed and chased all over the place all the time."

"True," admitted Dodge. "But now you've had a glimpse of an alternative – are you ever going to be satisfied with going back to the old routine?"

"That's what I can't decide," said Zak.

"Make decisions from the heart, and use your head to make it work out," said Dodge. He smiled. "Or don't."

"But am I being a wuss if I say no?" asked Zak, throwing himself onto the bench at Dodge's side.

Dodge looked carefully at him. "Are you worried that you won't be able to rise to the occasion?" he asked. "Because if you don't want to try because you're afraid of failing – then you're not the boy I thought you were."

Zak didn't respond.

The silence grew between them while Zak's brain churned. "I'd have the codename Quicksilver, if I joined," he said at last. "That's pretty cool."

"Yes, it is." Dodge rummaged in his pocket and pulled out a coin. Zak watched him as he held the silver coin up to the sun. It sparkled between Dodge's finger and thumb. "What are you doing, Dodge?" he asked.

"I'm performing an experiment," Dodge replied. He flipped the coin high. It caught the sunlight as it spun. Zak watched it rise and then fall into Dodge's open palm. Dodge's other hand slapped down on it before Zak could see which way up it landed.

"Heads you go for it – tails you don't," Dodge said, his eyes twinkling. "Come on, Zachary. Don't think about it. Which one do you wish it is?"

Zak stared at his friend's long bony hands.

A slow grin spread across his face.

He looked into Dodge's eyes and they both smiled.

"There's your answer," said Dodge.

Zak drew Colonel Hunter's pager out of his pocket and tapped in the contact code.

One thing was for sure – life was going to be very different from now on.

Turn the page for a sneak
preview of Zak Archer's
next mission:
The Tyrant King

CHAPTER **ONE**

Zak Archer was in the zone. Alert. Tireless. Wired.

He had never felt so alive in his life. Which was odd, considering how many people were out to get him.

Dawn had just broken. He was on the outskirts of the town. He had almost reached his objective.

Almost.

He dived for cover then belly crawled to a low wall, his backpack bouncing on his shoulders.

He crouched behind the wall and checked his Mob.

Things looked good.

So far.

The Mob was a smartphone used by British Intelligence. It was slim, oval and silvery, with an 80GB capacity. Cutting-edge technology. Zak pinched and flicked and the on-screen map expanded, showing the town in more detail.

A blue pulse showed his position. A red dot revealed his target. A yellow line ran along the shortest route between the two points.

Zak tried to stay calm and focused, but his heart was beating fast. It was a cool, overcast morning, but sweat was running down his forehead.

This was all happening too soon. He wasn't ready for it. Colonel Hunter had made a big mistake asking him to undertake this mission. He'd fail – and that would be it.

Done. Finished.

No! Stop thinking like that.

He pulled off his backpack and opened it. He took out the snakescope, a nifty gadget which looked like a conical pair of binoculars with a flexible cable attached to the front. Great for seeing around corners.

He kneeled and fed the cable over the top of the wall, twisting the dials as he looked through the twin eyepieces. A magnified circle roved across the deserted streets.

No sign of life. But it was creepy to know that there

were enemies hidden somewhere out there, waiting for the opportunity to get the drop on him.

Zak had undergone eleven weeks of intensive physical training since joining Project 17's fast-track course. It had been gruelling and relentless, and there were plenty of nights when he'd crashed out in his bunk bed, aching in places he never knew existed.

And now he had to make use of every trick he'd learned, or Project 17 would be down one agent and his new life would be over as soon as it had started.

No pressure, then.

He turned and put the snakescope into his backpack. Fitting the pack over his shoulders, he leaned against the wall. He closed his eyes and focused on his breathing.

Go on four.

One . . . two . . . three . . . GO!

He darted up and over the wall, running hard, arms pumping, feet skimming the tarmac. Part of his training had been about learning to control his ability to get into the zone.

The zone.

The zone had always been there, although it had never had a name till he'd met the young agents who formed the branch of British Secret Services called Project 17.

The zone was a place where the gears between his

brain and his muscles meshed. The zone was a place where he could outrun the wind. The zone was the best place in the world.

Zak heard the whine of a bullet and the sharp skip as it ricocheted off the ground at his heels.

They had found him.

Even in the zone, he couldn't outrun a sniper's bullet.

He looked around, seeking new cover.

A window was open – no more than thirty centimetres – but it was enough. He bounded over a low stone wall, across soft earth and, arms pointed like a diver's, through the narrow gap.

He rolled across bare floorboards, limbs tucked in, head down, letting his momentum carry him to the far wall.

Then he sprang up, listening for movement over the hammering of the blood in his temples.

Booted feet. Running fast. Coming closer.

He was out of the door and halfway up a staircase almost before his brain could catch up with him. He raced along a hallway to a back room, pulled the window open and peered down. There was the sloping roof of an outhouse beneath him, then a bare stretch of earth, a fence, and another row of houses.

Zak jumped onto the windowsill and let himself

drop, sliding down the roof. He caught the gutter with both hands, boosted himself off, then somersaulted onto hard-packed earth and started running again the moment his feet hit. Up and over the fence and into a narrow alley.

That was when he heard the distant throb of helicopter rotors.

Wow. They really were throwing everything at him.

A black Humvee skidded to a roaring halt at the end of the alley. Blocking his way out.

Zak knew he was almost out of options. But not quite. He ran towards the vehicle, gathering speed, his mind sharp.

He launched himself into the air, kicking out so his feet struck the car door just as it was being opened. There was a yell as the door crashed shut. His momentum lifted him. He landed with both feet on the roof of the Humvee, then sprang forwards, hitting the ground shoulder first. Rolling. On his feet again and heading away at top speed.

He heard shouting. A bullet zinged, striking sparks off a raised walkway directly ahead.

He snatched at the metal railings and slid through on a cushion of air. Rolling across paving stones. Up again. Running across an open courtyard between tall buildings. People in black were coming at him from all sides now. Five or six of them, only eyes and mouths visible through black masks.

Zak jumped onto the top of the first of a row of concrete bollards, then bounced from one to another along the whole row as his pursuers tried in vain to grab him out of the air.

No chance!

He sprang from the top of the last bollard, using every ounce of muscle power to boost himself up onto a high wall. He snatched at the top, his feet striking the brickwork, propelling him up and over onto a flat tarred roof.

He raced to another wall and scaled it at speed. But he was running against the skyline now – an easy target. And he could see the black helicopter gliding towards him like a high-tech mosquito.

He had to get off that roof and quickly.

He jumped again, aiming for the wall of an adjacent building. He flexed his legs and bounced backwards and forwards between the walls of the two buildings as he plummeted to the ground.

He landed well, absorbing the impact with bent knees, and continued down the long alley.

Zak took out his Mob and flicked to find the map again.

The blue pulse and the red dot were nearly touching. He had almost hit the target.

Now speed would have to give way to stealth.

He dipped into his backpack and pulled out a Taz – an electronic device designed to deliver an electric shock. It looked like a slim black torch. He flicked a switch and a red spot lit up.

The Taz was fully charged.

He edged along the wall and shot a glance around the corner. There was a single guard at the door.

Zak moved closer, silent as a ghost.

It was no good. The man heard him. He turned, raising his automatic machine gun, eyes fierce through the black ski mask.

Nothing to lose now.

Zak hurled himself forwards, gripping the Taz like a knife. He cannoned into the man, aiming the Taz at the man's neck as they both tumbled to the ground.

But he missed his mark. The man was twice his size and weight. He threw Zak off easily and sent him flying so that he landed in a dizzy heap.

He rolled onto his back and saw the man looming over him, silhouetted against the white sky.

"Not this time, kid," he said, aiming the gun.

Zak flung out his arm, flicking the switch on the

handle of the Taz. A pair of micro-wires snaked out, the twin barbed electrodes digging into the man's thigh. The Taz hummed and vibrated with power as the man collapsed on the ground.

Then Zak was on his feet. He pulled the gun from the man's hands and threw it aside. The man would be up again the moment the electric charge ran out. He had only a few seconds.

He raced up the steps to the entrance of the target building. It was an office block. He ran into a wide, empty foyer.

He saw the thin tripwire a thousandth of a second before his ankle hit it. He stumbled to a halt as the wire snapped.

"Oh, no! *No!*"

There was a loud muffled bang and suddenly the foyer was full of billowing grey smoke. Zak felt the floor fall away beneath his feet.

He went crashing down into darkness.

So close, and right at the end he'd walked into a booby trap.

Idiot!

He landed heavily, and lay gasping as the smoke swirled around him.

A figure emerged at his side. A heavy boot pressed

down on his chest.

Eyes glinted through a ski mask. A machine pistol pointed at him.

"Game over," said a voice.

There was a sharp crack and Zak felt an intense pain in his chest.